# Surrender To You

A Novel by

# C.S. Janey

Surrender To You

ISBN-10: 1491277610
ISBN-13: 978-1491277614

Cover Design by Cover Pub
(http://coverpub.samanthabagood.com)
Editing by Danielle Taylor
(http://authordtaylor.wordpress.com)

First Edition: September 2013
10 9 8 7 6 5 4 3 2 1

## DEDICATION

~*~

To my family and friends, who haven't once told
me that I'm insane for doing this.
I love you.

# ACKNOWLEDGMENTS

Thank you, first of all, to everyone in my life who has supported me to this point. I know you will continue to do so and nothing could possibly make me happier.

To my author friends that I talk to quite often - Danielle Taylor, Jennifer Howard, Christa Simpson - you three are the best friends a girl could ever have and I am honored to be called such! Thanks for all your advice and, more often than not, your ear when I'm rambling about things that most people might find embarrassing. ;)

To A.M. Khalifa - thanks for all your wonderful advice, your friendship and your input on the cover.

To the indie author community - you are all fantastic! I have never met such wonderful and supportive people in my life. It is amazing and I am proud to be a part of it.

To anyone who has offered me advice, or put advice up on the internet for authors to read, thank you. Your contribution is not going unnoticed.

To the readers and fans - thank you for supporting me by purchasing this! Thank you for reading and reviewing. Thank you for commenting and participating on my Facebook page, letting me know how much you are waiting for my book. Thanks, thanks, thanks! And I will try to write faster and procrastinate less in the future. ;)

To all the authors who responded to my list – thank you and I hope you find some great new readers! You will be listed in the future automatically, so no need to reapply every time I put out the sign-up.

# SURRENDER TO YOU

# CHAPTER ONE

*"Don't you miss me?"*

*"You know I do. But you're the one who left me..."*

*"I didn't want to, but you refused to let me in. You're the reason I left."*

*"Doesn't the pain I was in mean anything? I needed you and you walked out, even after all the promises you made."*

*"I just finally went the direction you told me to go every day. I simply gave you what you wanted. I left because you told me to."*

*"You leaving isn't what I wanted! You weren't listening! You never listened!"*

*"Maybe the problem was that you weren't saying anything worth me listening to." He turned and walked away with a shake of his head.*

*I slid to the floor, the knob of the kitchen cabinet slicing into my back, giving me another scratch on my body to join all the others that reminded me of the pain I couldn't manage to get rid of as I sobbed into my hands.*

The sound of my cell phone ringing jolted me out of the eerie dream I'd been having.

1

Rolling over, I picked up the flashing phone to see a random area code I had never seen before. Figuring someone from work could be calling me on a personal line, I slid the green phone icon across, putting the phone to my ear, shielding my eyes from the bright sunlight that filled my room at the same time.

"Hello?"

"Ellie?"

Oh, god. That voice. It haunted me in my slumber, but hearing it in for the first time in five long years sent my heart careening out of control. I hated my body for responding to it, for recognizing the need for him that I'd only admit to in my dreams.

*Say something, fool. He'd been the one to leave in the end, hadn't he?*

I cleared my throat and scowled even though he couldn't see me. "What are you doing calling me, Stefan? How did you even get my number?"

I'd changed it within hours after he'd left, never wanting to hear from him again. The jerk.

"Ellie, please don't be like that. I'm not..." His voice broke and I felt my heart twist as I realized something was wrong. "I'm not calling you because I want to."

Ouch. Well, he'd always been honest if nothing else.

"Why are you calling me then?"

"My mother..." I could hear him swallow, even as fear gripped my heart in acknowledgment of the bad news I had no doubt I was about to hear. "She's...dying and wants to see you. She begged me and I couldn't tell her no."

Shocked, I didn't know what to say.

Stefan's mother, Liliana, had been a second mother to me. Really, she'd been a second mother to a lot of people. The nicest woman in town, she was the mom everybody who didn't have a mom wished they had. She'd been best friends with my mother. Stefan and I became fast friends when our mothers ended up spending a lot of time together in the wake of both of their marriages falling apart.

Of course, one thing led to another with Stefan and I ended up falling madly in love with my best friend.

*Worst idea ever.* Our relationship disintegrated, much like the ashes left over from a bonfire, and our friendship came to an abrupt end. An end that sent me fleeing across the country to escape the excruciating pain in my heart.

The horrible reoccurring dreams affirmed how much I still suffered from the explosive end to us. The fact I continued to dream about him tortured me day in and day out.

"Ellie? Are you still there?"

"Uh...yeah," I replied while rolling out of bed. "I'm not really sure I can get the time off..."

He let out a deep sigh and I knew it was of irritation. It was a sound I'd heard all too often near the end of our relationship and I winced. I had always been disappointing him then and it seemed nothing had changed.

"I figured that in five years you'd have changed, even a little, but I can see you're still just as selfish as always."

His statement pissed me off. He had a way of doing that to me. Nobody else could ever come close to making me burn with anger as he did.

"Yeah, because you're just mister perfect aren't you? I have a life and a job. You know, to pay my bills with? I didn't go to college and work my ass off to just lose my job because I need to immediately leave town!"

Now I was shouting. Taking a deep breath, I winced as he cursed on the other end.

"Look, I didn't call to fight. She wants to see you. The least you could do is come home to visit her. I'm sure your work would understand. All you need is the weekend."

They would if I explained. My boss loved me and he'd understand, but paying my bills had nothing to do with not wanting to go.

In truth, I didn't want to see Stefan. I didn't want to be near him because it meant I'd have to see his face and hear his voice in person.

But I couldn't let Liliana down. She'd been there for me when my world fell apart. She'd kept my secret even when it had broken her heart and I wouldn't let her down, even if her son had walked away when I'd needed him most.

"I'll be there as quickly as possible," I said softly, hanging up before he could reply.

~*~

Knowing exactly who had given him my phone number, I dialed up my mother.

"Hello! Waller residence."

"Mother, it's me. How many times do I have to tell you to just look at your caller ID?" Ugh, I knew I sounded like a bitch but Stefan calling me had just ticked me off.

"I just pulled the phone out of my pocket and opened it, not even bothering to look. It's awfully early where you are, why are you calling me?"

"Oh, you know, because maybe you gave Stefan my number and he rang me up this early?"

"Ah."

I'm sure that if it were at all possible, steam would have come shooting out of my ears. "Ah? All you have to say is 'ah'? Why did you give him my number?"

"He said that his mother insisted he call and tell you. I kept trying to tell you myself but you are always so busy, so I figured maybe you'd answer the phone if it were from an unknown number…"

When her voice trailed off, I felt annoyed. She always acted as if she were inconveniencing me and even though she wasn't, I couldn't seem to convince her otherwise. Then again, I had moved to the other side of the country so maybe I'd given off the impression I didn't want to be bothered.

"So you've known for how long and it takes him calling me for someone to tell me Liliana is sick?"

She scoffed. "If you'd have answered my calls, I'd have told you sooner. It's not exactly something I wanted to leave on voicemail."

"Well, work keeps me busy. Some days, I don't even get home until it's way too late there with the time difference and all. It's not like I don't try."

*Liar, you don't try. You were avoiding her phone calls*. I hated when my inner voice scolded me. As if I needed another reminder of what a failure I was at being a daughter and a friend. Well, at everything really but now was not the time for a pity party.

"Sure sweetie, I know."

5

I could hear the resignation in her voice and knew she just wanted the phone call to end. Much as she loved me, I'd been a pain in the ass for the last six years and she didn't know why. She'd given up trying to get through as well and just let me go.

It was probably the best thing she'd ever done for me, even if I couldn't find the words to tell her.

Sighing, I pulled out my luggage to start packing. "Where is she at? I'll have to go into work and tell them what's going on but I could be on a flight by the end of the day."

"Well, there was nothing left to be done. She's at home, with all her family there. I've been to see her a few times…try not to let your shock show when you see her. She is very emaciated."

Gulping, I blinked rapidly to rid the sudden surge of tears to my eyes. "H-how long?"

No doubt hearing the catch in my voice, my mother's voice softened. "The doctor said not long. She was given about three months to live just a month ago, but it doesn't look like she will last much longer."

I knew what she was saying. She was ready to die and chances were that Liliana simply waited for me to make my appearance.

That thought alone had the tears coming faster and I knew I had to get off the phone.

"Okay, I gotta go. I'll see you when I get there."

"Be safe, Elizabeth."

Hanging up, I couldn't prevent the sobs from coming full force.

I never talked to anybody from home after I took off, not even Liliana. My mother and I talked but

6

through the years, that had become less and less. I had wanted to distance myself from all of them.

Now, I was returning but not on my own terms. I needed to get there, deal with this and then leave as fast as possible.

Pulling myself together, I picked up the phone and made one final phone call to my boss, hoping that a phone call would suffice to excuse myself in case my trip needed to be extended.

The weekend stretched out before me, painful and torturous.

I needed to hold it together, no matter what.

~*~

As the plane touched down, I stared out the window, wishing my travels led me anywhere but where I grew up. That I wasn't coming back to say goodbye to Liliana. That I wasn't going to have to face Stefan again.

Clearing it with work had been easy. They loved me and they were sad to hear about Liliana, telling me to take all the time I needed. Even as I assured my boss I'd be back on Monday, he'd softly repeated the statement, making it clear that he knew my return may not be immediate.

I'd sent my mother a text message before the plane took off with my arrival time; she'd responded saying she'd be there to pick me up. I figured I would just rent a car, but she assured me I could use hers during the visit and I wasn't one to turn down an opportunity to save money.

Finally able to get off the plane, I sat until the initial rush of people had passed, then grabbed my carry on from above and exited. Letting out a sigh, I entered the boarding area and looked around for my mother's bright red hair. Not seeing her, I looked down at my phone and turned off airplane mode, seeing a text message pop up as I regained service.

"Looking for me?"

*Son of a...*

At the deep voice, shock and irritation flooded through me. Turning to my right, my eyes landed on Stefan Pierce standing there with his hands in his pockets, the scowl on his face at odds with the gleam in his dark blue eyes. I couldn't tell if he was happy to see me or royally ticked off. Probably the latter, since he'd no doubt been wrangled into coming to pick me up from the airport.

I, on the other hand, would be having a nice long chat with my mother when I got home.

"Nope, I wasn't. I guess I'm gonna be renting a car since the person who was supposed to pick me up didn't show."

Now it was his turn to be shocked and I had to hold back a smile as his mouth dropped open just a little. Before he could say anything, I started to walk away, heading toward baggage claim.

"Didn't you bother to check your text messages? Or did you just assume nothing ever changes?"

I stopped abruptly and whirled around. "Wow, you're a bright one aren't you? When would you have liked me to check my messages, on the airplane? Perhaps you didn't notice I was looking down at my phone about to do that very thing when you said 'looking for me' so arrogantly?"

He blinked. "I wasn't —"

"Yeah, you were. Now get lost."

I was being rude, but I didn't care. I didn't want to see him at his mother's house, let alone have him pick me up from the airport. What the hell had my mother been thinking? Did she want me to turn right around and go back to my apartment?

Stefan chose that moment to stalk toward me, stopping within inches of slamming into me and grabbed my upper arms with his hands.

"What's your deal? Don't you think I've got enough shit going on without you giving me attitude?"

Surprised by the gentleness of his grasp, which happened to be at odds with the muted irritation in his voice, I stood mute and really looked at him.

He hadn't changed much over the years. He had never been very athletic, preferring simple things like bike riding to playing sports and enjoyed conquering computer games in his spare time. At only five foot six, I'd always found his height perfect because I could still wear heels and not feel either too short or too tall next to his five foot ten frame. His dark red hair was closely cropped and a small smattering of freckles graced his nose.

It was then, while looking at his face, that I saw he hadn't shaved today - and the lines of worry that hadn't been there before. He didn't look as youthful, the years having taken their toll on him. But at thirty years old, he still looked pretty damned tasty.

*Ugh, did I really just admit that to myself?*

Lifting my arms, I pushed against his chest. "Get off me!"

He let go easily, the scowl returning to his face. "Apparently not. Get your bags and lets go."

Huffing, I crossed my arms and glared. "Screw you. I told you I'd get my own damn—"

Leaning in, his mouth inches from mine, he hissed. "Shut up and get your fucking bags. You aren't wasting money on a car all because you wanna be a spoiled little brat. Your mother told me to come get you and I'll be damned if I don't deliver you safe and sound like she asked me to."

Rendered speechless by the banked anger in his voice, I glanced around to see the baggage claim area almost empty and a cleaning lady staring at us with curiosity. Walking over to the belt and picking up my bags, I lifted my chin defiantly and headed toward the doors, holding my tongue.

Stefan said nothing else to me as he led me to his car, which certainly filled me with relief.

The only positive thing that had come out of this was that we would have our words on the way home and not in front of his mother.

Not really looking forward to it even with the upside, I placed my luggage in the trunk and slammed it shut.

With a glare at me, he climbed into the driver's seat and in one more act of rebelliousness, I climbed into the back seat.

# CHAPTER TWO

The long thirty-minute drive ahead of us was going to be really slow if Stefan tortured me by being quiet.

While waiting for him to speak, I realized he had no intention of speaking first. Instead, he would use my aversion to silence to goad me into saying something. Probably an apology for my behavior but if that was his hope, he'd have better luck running for office.

Sighing exaggeratedly, I shifted in my seat, trying to get comfortable. I had a feeling that my inability to relax inside his vehicle had less to do with my accommodations and more with my ire at the man in the front seat ignoring me.

Five whole minutes passed and the itch to speak wouldn't go away, so I gave into the urge even though I knew I'd regret it.

"If you hate me this much, why did you agree to come get me?"

The car was dark so I couldn't tell if he was looking at me, but his response came swift and soft. "I don't hate you, Ellie. Even if I wanna wring your neck, I could never hate you."

11

"Really? You sure fooled me. Both in the past and just back there at the airport. I saw the look in your eyes."

His laugh, deep and rumbly, caught me off guard and made my stomach flip. Just as I remembered it, which only made this that much worse. I wanted to close my eyes and just disappear as thoughts of wrapping my arms around him to hold him close swirled in my head.

I hated the feeling, inconvenient and unwanted at this point.

"I'm glad I could be a source of amusement for you," I bit off, glaring at him even though he couldn't see me, trying to make myself feel better. Surely being mean and rude would be better than giving into the urge to touch him.

"You are surely mistaken about that look, honey," he said with another chuckle, taking the exit off the highway.

"I am not your honey!"

"No, you're definitely not at this moment. I didn't think it was possible but you might even be more bitter now than right before you skipped town."

Now it was my turn to laugh.

"Are you fucking kidding me right now? How would you know I skipped town since you left first!"

"I don't kid. You know why I left, you're just too damned stubborn to admit it to yourself."

"You left because you couldn't deal with real emotions. You were a coward."

He said nothing, pulling into an empty lot a few minutes later to park. Switching on the overhead light, he took off his seat belt and turned around to face me, lifting one brow. "Really? I was the coward

Ellie? Who was the one who told me day after day 'go, leave, you don't really want me, I don't believe you love me' etcetera? Why do I get shit for the crappy way you treated me every single day for a year?"

My pulse took off, heart slamming in my chest, and I knew I couldn't back down now. I'd teased the lion out of his cage and now it was all going to blow up in my face.

*Way to go, Ellie. Brilliant.*

"I don't know what the hell you are talking about." Damn my faltering voice. "I was depressed and you left me. We barely talked and were supposed to be planning a wedding and you just shut me out."

"No!" Stefan yelled, smacking his hand against the seat and causing me to jump. "You shut *me* out, Ellie! You walked around like a damn zombie and expected me to just act like everything was normal! What the hell was your problem? After all this time, if you wanna act like this, tell me what your fucking problem was!"

Tears clogged my throat. I couldn't answer him; it just wasn't that simple.

I shook my head, refusing to answer. In an extra effort to escape the heat in his gaze, I turned my head to stare out the window.

"That's what I thought," he muttered, letting out a growl of frustration as he turned back around.

The uncomfortable silence I'd been trying to avoid arrived with a vengeance as he turned off the light and continued the drive.

I should have just kept my mouth shut but around him, that had always been difficult. Especially when all I'd wanted from him was for him to love me

13

unconditionally. I knew now it didn't exist and therefore, would never happen.

The next words he spoke came as he pulled into my mother's driveway. "You should come by the house at eleven. Try not to be late. You can disappoint me all you want, but you will *not* disappoint my mother. And try to be civil. She doesn't need to hear this bullshit." His hands gripped the wheel tight, even as his words came out soft, almost pleading.

"I don't think I'm the one who needs to learn to control my temper," I couldn't resist retorting. His high and mighty attitude was getting on my last nerve and I didn't have many left at this point. "You always were the hothead."

"That's rich coming from you. At least I have a heart."

His words stung, poking at the very heart he denied me having. I knew if I said anything in return, I'd say something I regret.

Getting out of the car, I closed my door as the trunk popped open. Stefan didn't bother getting out of the car and I was glad for his stubbornness. It only made it easier to get back to ignoring him.

Slamming the lid shut the same way I had at the airport, I picked up my bags and stalked up to the door.

I didn't dare look back, yet I didn't hear his car pull away until I stepped inside.

~*~

I arrived at Liliana's house at exactly eleven-oh-one.

Yep, my actions were childish but after his parting words the previous evening, I just wanted to irritate him even more.

I didn't have a heart? He hadn't seemed to think such a thing when we'd first met. He was just trying to hurt me and wouldn't succeed. I'd be here for Liliana and then I'd leave, never having to think of him again.

Problem was, I wasn't all that sure he would be willing to leave my dreams that easily.

Walking up the steps, the door opened as I reached it. His sister Penelope - or Penny, as she'd often reminded me to call her - stepped into the doorway and gave me a soft smile.

"Elizabeth, how are you?" As she pulled me into a hug, I tried not to stiffen up in surprise. "Mother will be happy to see you."

"I'm okay," I replied as she released me, smoothing my blouse back into place. "Is she awake?"

Once I'd stepped inside, Penny shut the door, nodding solemnly. "Follow me."

It had been a long time since I'd been inside this house.

Five long and lonely years, to be exact.

Perhaps the most disturbing thing to me was that nothing had changed inside the house, yet it felt different. Most likely it was the fact I had become a different person, changed in many ways from the girl who'd come crying for help. This house had been my safe haven, until it had housed the biggest secret of all. I'd become a burden to it, the walls that kept my secrets and now, the only other person who'd understood it all lay in bed dying.

As we reached Liliana's room, I wondered for the first time if she had felt the weight of my secret all these years too.

Penny opened the door and stepped back. Walking through, I noticed that she didn't join me just as I spotted Stefan standing over by the window. Turning at the sound of me clearing my throat, he glanced at the bed before looking back at me.

"I will wait outside," he declared, walking past me without another word and out the door.

I approached the bed and sat in the chair. Then my eyes met Liliana's and I grabbed her hand with mine.

Squeezing her hand, I sniffled and willed the tears to wait until I was alone. "I'm here."

She gave me a weak smile and squeezed my hand back, albeit weakly.

"You...are still...as pretty...as always. I'm glad...you're here."

The words came out in between short breaths and I tried to look past the obvious agony she was in. "You don't have to talk," I assured her. "I know you must be in so much pain. I'm sorry for not calling..."

Right now I truly was and I hated myself. She had done so much for me and yet once I'd left, I'd never called her, not once.

"Don't...worry. I...understood. But you have...to tell him. He...deserves...to know."

My eyes filled with tears as I shook my head, trying to deny the emotion the mere thought induced. "I can't."

"That is my...final wish. That...you two...would make up. You...owe me."

Closing my eyes, I couldn't speak. I didn't know what to say. Five years wasn't long enough. In my

16

mind, not even twenty years would be enough and the pain would be a fresh wound the very moment the words left my mouth. I'd done so well at piling other crap on top of it, at making sure those memories would never hurt me again. She asked too much.

"How could you ask this of me? You know how much it killed me…it still kills me."

"I love you…and him. You both…deserve happiness. Quit…being a fool."

"Lily…" Though I tried to sound firm, my voice cracked under the weight of her demands. "Please, I—"

"Don't. I will tell…if you don't."

At this she closed her eyes. As I released her hand and placed it gently by her side, Stefan spoke from behind me.

"What was my mother talking about?"

Standing up, I took a deep breath and walked to the door without answering him.

He followed me and closed the door, taking my arm in his and steering me up the steps to the second floor. The touch of his hand on mine had me sucking in a breath and I tried to appear unaffected.

"Boy, you've gotten brave, haven't you?" I asked sarcastically and he glared, directing me into an empty room and shutting the door behind us. "Get your hands off of me!"

"I've only got one hand on you, but I can use the other to spank your ass if you don't shut up, if that's what it would take."

Mouth dropping open, I gaped at him. A beat later, I gasped. "You wouldn't dare."

"Try me."

Quickly shutting my mouth, I swallowed my smart-ass retort and jerked my arm out of his hand.

"Now...tell me what she was talking about."

Averting my gaze - really, I wanted to look anywhere but at his eyes - I crossed my arms over my chest.

"No, Stefan. It is none of your business."

"Bullshit. I heard enough to know that you better tell me or she will, so out with it."

I did my best to give him an icy look as I met his eyes with mine. "Go ahead. I'm leaving the day after tomorrow, so I don't give a crap. It won't change a thing."

He took a step forward and I backed up. It wasn't long until I felt the wall against my back and he placed a hand on each side of my head, leaning in. Our faces were so close our mouths nearly met. When he spoke, I shivered, his minty breath tickling my lips.

"I'm not letting you leave until you tell me."

I knew he wasn't bluffing, yet I had no plans to back down, especially from Stefan. We were both stubborn and it showed. "Make me."

The words were out before I could stop them. His eyes widened, the dark blue depths flaring with a look I knew all too well even as his mouth split into a wide grin.

"You know me, never one to turn down a dare."

His right hand gripped my hair near the nape of my neck as his lips descended upon mine.

# CHAPTER THREE

Wrong. So wrong. We shouldn't be kissing.

The press of his lips upon mine after all these years set the pit of my stomach in a near nauseous swirl of excitement. I couldn't help myself though. It had been so long since I had felt his hungry mouth on mine.

Right now wasn't the time. His mother lay downstairs dying and here we were, about to make out in the room upstairs because I couldn't keep my mouth shut. It wasn't right, yet I couldn't pull away. I didn't want to stop him. His kiss was gentle - way more so than I thought possible considering how angry he had seemed with me since my arrival.

His desire, however, was apparent. While one hand gripped my hair firmly, the other slid down the side of my body, giving me goosebumps along my right side. He snaked his arm around my waist, pulling me flush against him. With an involuntary gasp from me, he took advantage and swooped in with his tongue.

With a moan, I relaxed my body, his answering groan accompanied with a tightening of the arm he had about my waist. Pushing me against the wall with his body, he ground against me and I brought my arms up to push him away.

"Oh no you don't," he growled against my mouth, releasing his grip on my hair and waist to grab my hands. Lifting my arms above my head, he gripped both wrists with one hand and held them there. "I'm not done making you talk yet."

His high-handed tactics pissed me off. "You bastard! You think you can just—"

He cut the words off with a punishing kiss, invading my mouth with an urgency I'd only felt from him during my dreams. I wanted to cry at the exquisiteness of these feelings I'd been missing all these years even as I wanted to kick him for making me feel that way.

With his free hand, he unbuttoned my blouse, shoving it open when the last one slipped through the buttonhole. Unhooking my bra with the expertise of a man well-versed in the bedroom, he cupped my breast in one hand, his palm hot against my skin. Moaning as he ran his fingers along the underside of my breast before pinching the nipple gently, I felt him chuckle into my mouth.

Stefan leaned in, using his weight to trap my body to the wall while I bucked against him to try and get free. Even though he was tall and lean, he wasn't weak by any means. I could feel the heat of his skin through his shirt, the fabric teasing my nipples as if asking them to come out and play.

Releasing my mouth, he lowered his head, licking a path from my throat to my nipple, taking it in his mouth and sucking on it. Letting out a soft cry, I bucked again.

"Stefan...please..." I looked down to find his eyes staring up at me while he rolled his tongue around my nipple, over and over again until my knees felt as if they would collapse beneath me. "We shouldn't...I shouldn't..."

At that, he nibbled lightly and a sob of desire escaped me.

He knew me, even after all this time. I wanted his touch, trusted it, even as I tried to deny my need.

I hated myself for wanting it, desiring it so much I didn't want to say no even though I should. Hating him for being the one to make me feel this way, the *only* one.

Unaware of my internal thoughts, he released my breast, his hand gliding down my chest and abdomen as his mouth moved to my other nipple, teasing it with the same devilishness as he had the other just moments before. With a quick motion, he undid the button of my jeans and unzipped them, sliding his hand smoothly into my panties as well. Standing up abruptly, he released my arms and grabbed my ass, thrusting me upward for better access.

Devouring my mouth with his, I responded with a ferocity I didn't know had been left in me, my fingers clawing at his shoulders as I tried to anchor myself.

I wanted him to touch me so badly. I wiggled as he slipped lower and lower, aching for the touch I'd denied myself for so long by not telling him my secret. I felt the tears streaming down my cheeks even as our tongues battled, the saltiness mixing in with the mint of his breath. I sobbed harder, incapable of pulling away and even more unable to stop this. I was starved for his touch, desperate enough to not care about the consequences.

His hand finding me was my undoing.

With a few skillful touches, I cried out at the sweetness coursing throughout my body as he gave a triumphant and utterly male chuckle. No doubt he was proud of himself and he should be. Nobody knew me and my body like he did. Years of familiarity had given him an advantage and he knew it.

As he pulled his hand out, he let me down gently before stepping away. I gripped the side of my blouse together and glared at him.

"I bet you're mighty proud of yourself right now, aren't ya?"

*Oh, that's brilliant Ellie. The man gives you the first orgasm you've had in six years and you gotta be snarky? Nice.*

Stefan's face closed up as I threw a withering look at him. Then he responded with a cocky grin and I knew I'd done it now.

"Damn right I am! I don't hate you, Ellie. If I did, I wouldn't be caught in the same room with you, let alone with my hand down your pants. Now, tell me what you and my mother were talking about."

"Fuck you!" I wasn't telling him a thing.

With a quick perusal of me from head to toe, he shook his head. "No thanks. Now get dressed and when you've calmed down enough, come to the kitchen. Mother wanted you involved in her final preparations so be prepared."

Like I'd been hit in the face with cold water, I could do nothing but gape at the man as he walked out the door.

~*~

I took my time before attempting to head downstairs. Pulling myself together enough to face him and his five siblings took an effort. Part of me wanted to walk up to him and smack him for his treatment of me just now, so I needed to calm down first. Not to mention, I'd let him touch me. If I'd have said no, he would have stopped but I hadn't because I'd wanted him to touch me.

That's how it had always been with us. Hot and heavy...and angry. Anger had seemed to invade whatever room we'd been in during the last year of our relationship and the actions of both us in that room suggested that hadn't changed one iota.

Truth is, I missed how things were before they went all wrong. As I slowly descended the steps, my mind drifted back to the day before he left to go abroad that summer...

*"Hey Stefan, come on in!" I heard my roomie greet him and I hurried to finish applying my mascara. "She's in the bathroom."*

*"What's new? She always takes forever," he replied with a laugh as the door closed. "I'll just go to her."*

*"Nah, she'll be out in just a moment. You want a drink?"*

*Grace was just that - full of grace. And she was also such a sweetie. She had been thrilled when Stefan and I had finally 'gotten together' because, according to her, best friends always made the best boyfriends and husbands. Her whole family was full of marriages of people who had done the same thing and she swore by it.*

*Sailing into the room, Stefan's face lit up at the sight of me and my heart clenched almost painfully. He'd always been happy to see me, but ever since his proposal three months ago, it was as if his love grew every day. I didn't know what to do with it but I appreciated every moment. I had loved him for ages and for him to return it just made me the happiest I'd ever been.*

*"You ready to go, Ellie?"*

*He was the only person who called me that. I always introduced myself as Elizabeth to everyone and they stuck with that. He'd never liked it though and had given me a nickname instead, saying it suited me way more. I loved that we had that between us though and the sound of my nickname on his tongue always turned me on.*

*Walking over and putting my arm through his, I nodded. "I'm always ready for you!"*

*With a chuckle he leaned in and stole a kiss.*

"Earth to Ellie!"

Jumping at the sound of his voice, I looked up to find Stefan with hands on his hips, one brow raised.

"What do you want?"

His amusement disappeared, replaced with a frown and punctuated with a sigh.

"Are you all right? You were just staring at the floor and I called your name like three times."

Great. Apparently, I'd stopped at the end of the steps and just stood there, looking like a fool as I thought about the old us. Wonderful.

"Yeah, I'm fine. I was just trying to figure out when you turned into such a prick."

24

"I think it was a little after you turned into such a bitch," he retorted hotly as his ears turned pink, giving away his embarrassment. "If you're done taking your damned time, we're waiting for you in the kitchen!"

"Ass," I muttered as I walked past him. When he didn't shoot back at me, I figured he hadn't heard my reply.

He entered the kitchen right behind me and five heads turned in unison.

"I found her daydreaming at the end of the steps," he announced to his siblings, and as the heat rushed to my face, they laughed. "She looked pretty into it."

Rolling my eyes, I took a seat next to Penny. "Hi guys. Ignore him, he's just jealous it wasn't him making me daydream."

Liar, liar pants on fire. That was me right now. I wondered if the others in the room were capable of reading the blatant lies I knew were written all over my face.

Penny snickered even as her three brothers - Adrian, Evan, and Jerome - tried to hide their grins by ducking their heads. His other sister, Yvette, scowled at me. She hadn't liked me for a very long time though, so her lack of amusement didn't shock me.

"Well, Stefan, you and I have already spoken so I'm going to go sit with mom," Yvette said, leaving the room before anybody could respond.

No doubt she only did it to escape being in the same small space with me. I never quite knew why she'd stopped liking me but I suppose it mattered very little now. I didn't plan on being here long enough to care.

Stefan pulled up a seat in the empty space next to me around the center bar. Automatically shifting my legs to try and avoid touching him, I wasn't prepared for the shock of his hand on my leg, stilling my escape. My eyes clashed with his as he squeezed, his message delivered with stealth.

I wasn't going to get away from him from this time. He'd get his answer one way or another.

*Oh yeah? Watch me.*

No doubt seeing the dare in my eyes, he winked before turning to face the others.

"So, mom's final wishes are that she be cremated," he said softly. "She doesn't mind a wake but you know her, being put in the ground just wasn't something she ever desired."

I stiffened, the declaration of her final wishes news to me. She had told me otherwise years before.

"But, I..." Stefan glanced over at me with a questioning look as I tripped over my words. "W-when did she change her mind?"

They all stared at me then, the bewildered looks something that would perhaps have been amusing at another time.

"What are you talking about?" It was Penny who asked this, her eyes growing misty. "She told you she wanted to be buried? When was this?"

"Uh..." I had stuck my foot in my mouth this time. "Well, she...before I left...we had a discussion."

I knew my explanation was lame, but I couldn't go into detail without giving away more information than I wanted or desired to share.

Stefan pulled his hand away as if it were on fire, his voice clipped as he glared at me.

"When did you and mom have this discussion about death exactly? And why? That doesn't seem like something she'd discuss for no reason."

I didn't know why he was mad. Why they were all staring at me as if I grown another head all of a sudden.

"We...uh..." I stumbled over my words, my embarrassment growing with every second. "We talked about it after you left that summer. It was like, two months maybe?"

I knew exactly when it was. The day was etched into my mind permanently, never to be forgotten.

Pushing up from my chair, it screeched rudely across the floor as I hurried over to the door.

"I'm sorry. I shouldn't...I'm sure you all know her best. I...I have to go."

"Ellie!"

Ignoring Stefan's voice - and obvious irritation with me - I ran. And I didn't stop until I was driving away, silent tears streaming down my face as the memory of what had happened six years ago flooded over me.

# CHAPTER FOUR

*"Are you ready for a fun night out?"* Grace called out to me.

I stood in the bathroom, trying to finish putting on what little make-up I liked to wear - some mascara and eye liner. A few seconds later, we left our apartment and got into the car.

Stefan had been gone just over a week and I already missed him like crazy. We stayed in touch over Skype but not being near each other was way worse than I could have ever imagined. And his trip abroad would take the whole summer. Part of me just wished he missed me so much that he'd come home sooner than originally planned. I didn't know how I'd survive that length of time without him. Dramatic maybe, but that's how I felt.

Grace's answer was to go out and I couldn't find a good reason to say no. The drive to the club took nearly an hour, which was the nearest city to our small rural town, and we blasted music the whole way there. Nothing like a little prep work to prepare for the loud music in the club.

*After finding a spot to park and walking roughly ten minutes in our heels, Grace grabbed my hand and sailed to greet the bouncer at the door.*

*"Hey Billy! What's a girl gotta do around here to get in faster?"*

*As she batted her eyelashes at Billy, I rolled my eyes. Billy had a thing for her and she took great pains to keep him interested, but not let him into her pants. I had to give it to the girl, she was smooth.*

*"How 'bout a kiss, Gracie?"*

*Grace looked back at me and winked, to which I promptly made a gagging motion with my hand into my mouth. She giggled and turned back around, stepping up on her toes and kissing him square on the lips.*

*The people in line simultaneously laughed and booed, realizing she was bribing her way into the club. But it was over quickly and we were let through, Grace laughing like crazy.*

*Inside, the amount of bodies shocked me. Having only been here twice before, I walked behind Grace as she flitted her way through the club, greeting people by name. The loud music made it hard to hear so introductions were very scarce and eventually we made it up to the bar, where Grace ordered us some drinks.*

*"We're gonna have so much fun!" She screamed at the top of her lungs. I smiled back at her, unsure of her assessment with the situation. We were in near danger of being squished by all the bodies packed around the bar and I became afraid to move.*

*In truth, all I wanted right then was Stefan. I desired a quiet night at home, snuggling on the couch while watching a movie and an occasional*

29

*kiss. Touching and kissing that would lead to some awesome sex with my man.*

*Sighing, I picked up my drink as it was placed on the counter, nodding my thanks at the bartender. My plan was to only drink one because I wanted to be sober by the time we headed home, which would be at least four hours from now.*

*Grace grabbed my hand and pulled me into the crowd. Finding an open space, she held her drink high up in one hand, swaying her body back and forth as she stands close to me. Winking, she dances around me as I awkwardly try to mimic her actions, as I wasn't much of a dancer.*

*After a few dances, Grace went to get another drink and I moved to stand against the nearby wall. That's when I noticed the bouncer's buddy, Lawrence, staring at me. Giving him what I'd hoped was a 'keep your distance' look, I anxiously awaited for Grace to come back. Standing up on tiptoes, I saw her coming through the crowd and let out a sigh of relief. I had no desire to end up alone at any point this evening.*

*We began dancing again when a hot guy came up to Grace and asked her to dance with him.*

*"I don't want to be alone!" I yelled to her and she just smiled.*

*"You'll be fine! It's just one dance!"*

*I went back to standing against the wall, arms crossed as I watched Grace and the guy grind together on the dance floor.*

*Lawrence, seeing me standing all alone, must have believed I was up for a chat as he sauntered over to me.*

*"Well hey there, sexy. I've never seen you around here before." His words were slurred and when he smiled at me, I wondered how such an attractive man ended up to be such a sleazeball. The creep vibe from him was strong and I backed up.*

*"Yes, you have, Lawrence. I've been here before with Grace."*

*He looked confused for a second before he nodded. "R-right. I remember. You're much prettier than her, y'know. Billy is blind."*

*"I can't say I'm upset about that."*

*He grinned again, leaning against the wall. "Neither can I."*

*Unable to stop my eyes from rolling with annoyance, I pointed behind him. "Excuse me, I need to go to the restroom."*

*The smile left his face even as he nodded and I walked away.*

*When I came back out, he was nowhere to be found and I let out a sigh of extreme relief. I really didn't want to deal with that bullshit tonight. Looking for Grace and unable to find her, I approached Billy who now stood inside the doors in case of trouble.*

*"Hey Billy, you see Grace anywhere?"*

*Not really moving any muscles except the ones for his mouth, he replied, "Yep, she just went outside a few seconds ago for a smoke."*

*Ugh. I despised smoking and she only did it on the balcony of our apartment because the smell alone gave me a migraine. But I really just wanted to go home now, so I thanked him and headed outside. Looking to my left and right, I didn't see anyone.*

*The eerie quietness of the street started giving me a bad feeling and as I turned around to go back inside, a voice called out to me.*

*"Hey pretty girl, where you going?"*

*As I turned around to tell him off, something hit me in the side of the head and I blacked out.*

~*~

*I awoke in bed, confused.*

*Surrounded by darkness, I tried to figure out whose bed I could possibly be lying in. At the sound of soft crying to my left, I decided against turning my head that way, the ache in it almost unbearable.*

*Instead, I licked my lips and spoke. "W-where am I?" The words were softer than I'd intended, yet I knew I'd been heard as the person gasped.*

*"Oh god! Elizabeth, I was so worried!" Grace moved into my line of vision, her eyes red and swollen. "What the hell happened?"*

*I closed my eyes before opening them again slowly. "I don't...know. I got..hit in the head and...that's all I remember. Where am I at and how...did I get here?"*

*"I brought you to Stefan's mother. Billy came up to me saying that somebody had reported that you passed out in the alley and I was like what the hell was she doing outside by herself! I was gonna take you to the hospital but you woke up when we moved you and begged me not to, that you just wanted to go home."*

*I didn't remember that. How had I ended up in the alley?*

*She took my hand in hers and squeezed. "Since Stefan's mother is a nurse, I brought you here so she could check you out. I gotta go get her, she wanted to know when you woke up."*

*Leaving the room before I could reply, I scoured my mind. Who had hit me? And why?*

*Only a few moments passed before Liliana came into the room, her worried blue eyes - so like Stefan's that I wanted to weep with the wanting of him right now - sweeping me from head to toe. Grace stood behind her, wringing her hands.*

*"Good, you're awake. What the hell happened, Elizabeth?"*

*Licking my dry lips, I lifted one arm. "I don't know. I...nobody called...the cops did they?"*

*Grace nodded. "Billy did after we left, he has to for legal reasons. They will want to talk to you."*

*"No...I don't want to."*

*"Too bad," Liliana's voice was stern. "Nobody can just hit you in the head and get away with it."*

*"But I don't...remember anything. Can I get...some water?"*

*They hurried to get me some water. As I drank it, Liliana kept looking at me funny and I wanted to ask what was wrong but refrained. She then declared that her duty demanded she take me to the hospital so off we went. On the way there I begged her not to tell Stefan and she promised me even though I know she didn't want to.*

~*~

*Three weeks later, after the initial craziness had calmed down, I was sitting at the table with my head in my hands when Lily walked in.*

*"The police are going to close your case, if you can't give them something," she declared, taking a seat next to me.*

*"Well, there is nothing I can do. I absolutely don't recall anything. I can't make my brain work on their schedule."*

*She sighed, covering my hand with hers. "Are you sure you're all right?"*

*Looking at her with burning eyes, I could no longer hide the tears.*

*"My period is late."*

*Her eyes widened as she gasped. "Is it —?"*

*"No, I'm afraid it's not. I...think...something happened to me when I was knocked out," I wailed, the sobs coming full force and I felt her arms close around me. "I don't know what to do. I am on the pill, this wasn't supposed to happen!"*

*"I looked you over...your clothes weren't torn or anything, but nobody knows how long you were lying there." I could hear the tears in her voice now. "You were missing for a good thirty minutes, at least, Grace said."*

*The fact she'd taken me to the hospital even though I hadn't wanted to go had been a good thing, since the police required it for the report. The nurse had asked me a bunch of questions about the incident and I'd said no when she'd asked if I thought anything else had happened. I remembered nothing along with feeling fine and just wanted to get out of there. I never considered that something worse had happened after being knocked out.*

*"How could I miss that? How could I be so stupid? I should've known."*

*"You're not stupid! You had been hit in the head, you were fully dressed and no torn clothing. I should have encouraged you to get a rape kit done, even if you didn't think anything had happened. Have...have you taken a test?"*

*I shook my head. "No, I...wanted to talk to you first."*

*The look on her face said she knew exactly what I wanted to do if I was. "Well, let's get a test first, okay? Maybe the stress of the last few weeks is causing it."*

*Except it wasn't. And it didn't take me long to set up an appointment to have the pregnancy terminated. Liliana stayed by my side as they explained the risks and the procedure for taking the pills. A few days later, it was done and over with along with an STD test to make sure I was clean, with advise to come back in again months down the road to be extra safe.*

*I swore Liliana to secrecy. She begged me to let her tell Stefan, but I told her it was my business and I'd tell him in my own time.*

*That time never came.*

~*~

As my phone rang the next morning, I groaned at the unexpected noise and the bright sunlight streaming into the room. I'd imbibed too much alcohol the night before in a vain attempt to re-bury the memories and now I had a killer hangover. Reaching over and picking up my phone, I saw Stefan's number and instantly felt nauseous.

Stumbling out of bed, I made it to the bathroom as my body revolted. The phone stopped ringing only to start up again seconds later. Slowly making my way back to the bed, I answered.

"Hi."

"Ellie," was all he said, the tears in his voice meaning only one thing.

*I'm sorry.* The words stuck in my throat. They were superfluous anyway but I still felt as if I should say them.

I could hear him breathing as he waited for me to say something, anything.

"I..." What could I possibly say? I decided to go with practical. "When is the wake?"

He coughed, the emotion roughening his words as he spoke. "The wake is tomorrow night at seven with the funeral on Tuesday morning at ten."

"Wow. That's much sooner than I expected." Then, his words clicked with me. "Wait, a funeral? I thought..."

"You were right," he interrupted. "Told me last night that she'd written it all down and had it all set to go as soon as..."

*As soon as she'd found out she was dying.*

Yeah, I wouldn't want to finish that sentence either.

"I wish she would have told you her plans," I whispered. "I didn't mean to upset you guys yesterday."

"Not your fault."

There wasn't much else I could say, his curt replies hurting me even though I knew he grieved for his mother. "I'll be there."

He hung up without responding, which I completely deserved.

I'd never done well with death. To me, it was just the end of a natural cycle. I'd always been a private person and crying in front of others wasn't something I would do. I felt awkward at emotional times because I never appeared to 'react the right way' which had been one of the big issues after the 'incident' as I liked to call it now.

Letting out a breath I hadn't realized I'd been holding, I dialed my boss to let him know I wouldn't be back to work until mid-week.

~*~

The day of the funeral came, foggy with cloudy skies. We all stood outside with our jackets on, umbrellas nearby in case it rained surrounding the casket as the ceremony progressed.

I stood next to my mother, who wept into a tissue and had her arm around me as if I were the one who needed the comfort.

Stefan stood on the other side, surrounded by his siblings as they all huddled together, arms around one another. I couldn't see his face as he was rather focused on the casket in front of us.

Liliana's wishes were to be buried at the local cemetery. Her ex-husband, Richard, stood next to his children with a stony look on his face. Yvette had moved a little earlier to stand next to him, and they murmured a bit. Or rather, she did most of the talking. He kept shaking his head and she just looked more pissed off by the minute.

As the ceremony ended, everyone started to

leave and I looked over to Stefan, only to have Yvette suddenly blocking my view.

"I can't believe you actually bothered to show your face here, you couldn't even stay to help the other day!"

I took a step backward as my mother stepped in front of me.

"Your momma would be ashamed that you're being so disrespectful at her service. This is not the place."

She laughed, her eyes glaring daggers at me.

"Doesn't anybody ever tell you off? You're such a selfish bitch and I'm so glad you ran my brother off."

"What is your problem?" I hissed back at her, trying to lower the general volume of the conversation to avoid attracting Stefan's attention. "And you got it all wrong. He walked out."

"Yeah, after *you* pushed him away. What did you do while he'd gone abroad huh? Did you just scheme your way into our mom's life so she'd leave you the house? Then decided to make him leave you since you got what you wanted?"

Jerking my head back, my eyes flew to my mothers that were also filled with shock.

"What the hell are you talking about? I didn't do anything to your mother and I certainly didn't know she left me the house!"

Richard stepped over and grabbed Yvette's arm, tugging on it.

"Walk away, Yvette. You're making a fool of yourself," he told her with a nod in my direction. "My apologies, Elizabeth."

Yvette threw a final frown at me before

stalking off, leaving me bewildered by the news and her attitude. Her father shook his head in annoyance as I stared at him.

"Why in the world did Liliana leave me the house?"

Richard shifted his weight, uncomfortable as he took my hand in his.

"Liliana...she was adamant that you needed a place to call home. I tried to convince her that she'd anger the kids but the only one who seems mad at her decision is Yvette. Elizabeth...she loved you and I promise you, I'm all for you having the house. She and I have always been friendly..." He trailed off and glanced over at my mom as he stopped.

Oh. I see. He knew my secret. But why had Lily told him and not Stefan?

He must have seen the question in my eyes.

"She always said that you'd do the right thing eventually. That when you did and things worked out with Stefan..."

I shook my head. "I don't think that will happen, but I appreciate it. Does Yvette want the house, because she can—"

He cut me off. "No, sadly, she can't. The terms were that you get the house, or it goes up for sale and the proceeds go to Liliana's favorite charity. So don't let her convince you otherwise because all the kids signed off on it."

"Why would she sign off if she wanted it?"

"Her mother threatened to cut her off. She just wants something to bitch about, I guess."

"She just doesn't want me to have it, you mean."

He smiled sheepishly. "Yes, but don't let that

stop you. You'll be sent the paperwork to sign off on. You should take it to a lawyer. Assuming, that is, that you don't want to sell it?"

At that, my mother piped up. "Don't be silly, Richard! Of course she doesn't want to sell Liliana's house."

As he nodded, she looked over at me. "We'll talk later. I'm gonna walk Richard to his car. You should..."

Jerking her head in Stefan's direction, my mother put her arm on Richard's and they walked away.

I stood rooted to my spot, watching as Stefan stood near the grave, alone.

Wanting to go to him, but not. Wanting to kiss him, yet unable to gather up to courage to do so.

He must have felt my eyes on him, glancing up and staring straight at me.

In that moment, I knew that Stefan wanted me and it would never change. The hungry stare on his face, in his eyes, and in his stance said it all.

He considered me his. He loved me and always had. I'd been the blind one, foolish enough to let my fears tear me away from the people who had done nothing but care about me. If I talked to him, he'd try to make me stay.

Especially now that his mother had given me her house.

I didn't know how to feel. I wanted him and yet, I didn't. Going back wasn't possible. You couldn't undo the past. And the look in his eyes terrified me. Because I recognized it. The look same as the one he wore in my dreams, even as he denied me with his every breath.

But it wasn't him denying me. I did that to myself.

And when he smiled at me, I knew that he knew my thoughts, which only alarmed me even more.

So I did what I always did best. I nodded at him, turned around and walked away to take the first flight home.

# CHAPTER FIVE

Putting my bag down just inside the door, I kicked off my heels and walked toward the kitchen to pour myself something to drink.

Work was exhausting, but it'd been a week since I'd gotten back and I was more grateful than ever for the way it kept me busy.

Too busy to think, too busy to wonder where Stefan was and what he was doing.

Well, until I got home, where he entered my mind the moment I walked in my door apparently.

Sighing, I quickly stripped off my shirt and walked toward the bedroom. I'd get a drink once I got into something more comfortable since I didn't plan on getting off my couch until bedtime.

Putting on a tank top and some soft pajama pants, I was heading back to the kitchen when a loud knock came at my door.

"Just a second!" I yelled. The knocker didn't answer so I played it safe. Upon reaching the door, I looked through the peephole and gasped.

Swinging my door open, I glared at a soaking wet and quite angry-looking Stefan standing on my doorstep.

Giving my head a little shake to prepare myself, I breathed deeply, still glaring and asked, "What in hell are you doing here? And how did you get my address?"

"It was on your luggage tags, Miss Brilliant," he retorted. "Are you going to let me in so I can dry off?"

I stepped back. I knew he wasn't going to go anywhere and I didn't think I could handle his hands on me right now.

Shutting the door as he walked past me and into my front entryway, I couldn't help but stare at his back. The white button down shirt, thanks to the rain, had gone completely transparent and his equally wet jeans sculpted to his body like nothing I'd ever seen on him before. I had to refrain from licking my lips, fearing it would mess up the scowl I kept on my face when he was around.

Call it a defense mechanism, but if he knew how much he turned me on with the mere sight of him, he'd take advantage of that and I'd be screwed all over again. Literally.

Grinning at my unintended pun, I let out a giggle and he whirled around to face me with heat in his gaze.

"What's so damn funny?"

"You...You look like a drowned animal," I lied. "It's hilarious. I've never seen you so less put together."

He stalked up to me then and got in my face.

"I'm not amused. You literally left hours after the funeral. What the fuck is wrong with you?"

Oh, shit. I wiped the grin from my face and glared up at him defiantly. "I was done there and I had a job to get back to. If you don't like how I deal with my grief, you can go to hell!"

*Oh, yeah and I wanted to get away from you and your intense stare before I let it convince me to strip naked for you.* I didn't dare say that out loud.

"I'm already in hell, Ellie. You didn't stay, so I've come to you because I want answers."

My face heated, the intensity of his stare making me drop my eyes even though I knew I shouldn't. "Well," I steeled myself, squaring my shoulders. "You can't have them! Why are you even here? Don't you have a job or something?"

"Bullshit. I took time off, I had it coming to me. And I already told you why I'm here," he growled. "Dammit, can't I have a fucking towel or something?"

Grateful for the opportunity to walk away, I opened the hallway cabinet and pulled out a towel. Re-entering the living room, I stopped short at the sight of Stefan's bare chest. He used his shirt to try and rub his head dry and the muscles in his arm held me transfixed. And his chest... he wasn't ripped, but I didn't see an ounce of fat anywhere.

Who was this buff man? I guess I should have noticed his strength when he'd held me up against the wall in that room upstairs at his mothers house. My body began responding to the memory, thighs clenching as my nipples tightened. It was too bad I'd marked him as off-limits to myself because I really wanted to jump his bones right now.

Clearing my throat to make my presence known, he glanced up just as he started using the shirt to dry his chest. The towel gripped in my outstretched hand, I watched, my body stiff, as he took the few steps forward to grab it. Then the man had the audacity to wink at me while doing so.

"Thanks, honey."

I didn't bother correcting his use of the endearment. My emotions were already raw, the sight of him half naked in my living room throwing me for a loop. I hadn't expected him to follow me, to want answers so badly that he'd come all this way to squeeze them out of me.

He had come all this way *for* me.

Attempting to make friendly conversation, I put my hands behind my back and looked down at the floor. "So, I guess you work out huh? When did that happen?"

"About a month after you left. I thought maybe if I buffed up, I'd find me another girlfriend quick."

Ouch. I guess I deserved that. But I could give as good as I got and I did so with ferocity in my voice. "Looks like that didn't work out so well for you, considering you're still single and all."

Stefan's bark of laughter had me looking up from the floor and to his face. It didn't stop there though.

With lightning speed, he wrapped his arm around my waist and pulled me against his body. Stiffening, I put my arms against his chest and pushed, but as I'd guessed, the effort was futile.

He had me trapped. He'd come all the way to my place and I'd been dumb enough to let him in.

"Relax," he suggested gently, the deep, velvety soft timbre of his voice sending shivers down my spine. "I know you want me."

A thread of desire twisted through me at his words. I ignored it.

Instead I scoffed and let out a laugh of my own. "You wish."

Dropping the towel to the floor, he wrapped his hand in my hair and pulled slightly, baring my neck but keeping his eyes on mine.

"Knock it off, Ellie. Just admit you want me and I'll let you go."

"I don't believe you," I whispered shakily. "You followed me all the way home. I thought I'd escaped then."

"Mistake number one," he murmured back. "Tell me you want me."

"No," I said, even though my statement was false and we both knew it. "I don't want you. Let me go and leave me be."

"Liar. Now it's I who doesn't believe you."

Sliding his hand down to my ass, he yanked me flush to his frame, his arousal evident against my belly.

"I want you Ellie. I've always wanted you and I've finally decided to do something about it. I've spent five *long* years craving you and your delicious body. I'll be damned if I'm going to pass up a chance to have you all to myself, to convince you that we're good for each other. Meant for each other."

I whimpered, unable to do anything as the emotion in his voice elicited butterflies in my tummy and a speeding up of my heart.

Trouble with a capital T stood in my apartment, holding me captive in his embrace, and I wasn't sure I wanted to escape.

~*~

Here in the familiar warmth of his arms, I wasn't sure what to do. What to say.

I didn't know his objective here. He wanted me? I couldn't figure out *why* he wanted me when he'd already had me. Six years ago, he'd proposed and I'd say yes, with every intention of becoming his wife. Of sharing our futures together.

And while I suffer with all my pain, pain I couldn't share even though I'd tried, he'd walked away.

Why did he his words and wishes now deserve any consideration?

*Because you owe him and you know it. You should have told him.*

Scowling at my own thoughts, I relaxed my arms and Stefan chuckled, releasing my hair and hugging me close.

"Hey Ellie?"

His breath flitted over the shell of my ear, ticking me, and making me tense up again. "Hmm?"

"You think I could get my clothes off and washed?"

Pulling back in alarm, I gaped at his bold assumption. "What do you mean? You aren't staying here!"

He arched one perfectly curved brow and let me go slowly. When my feet touched the floor, I shoved off of him and pivoted around, dropping onto the couch only a few feet away.

"Yeah, actually, I am. I figure if I stay at a hotel, you'll find lots of ways not to see me."

He was right, damn him!

"So? You can't just invite yourself to stay. I...I like my privacy."

It was the truth. I valued my secrecy now more than ever. Plus with him around, I feared nothing would ever get done and I wasn't sure how long I could put up a defense against his effortless seduction. And if I were completely honest with myself, I didn't want him to ever leave. If he stayed here with me, Stefan might just win.

I heard the door open and craned my neck to see what the heck he was doing.

My tiny hope that he'd left had been in vain, as he pulled a piece of luggage inside from the hallway. Sighing, I knew getting rid of him was going to be a pain in the ass unless I wanted to call the cops, but that would just be unforgivable.

I wanted him to leave, not to end up in a jail cell.

Instead, I'd just make his visit here a living hell. Maybe if I disturbed his sleep enough, he'd get fed up and leave.

"Fine," I relented. "You can sleep on the couch. The washer and dryer are in the far corner of the kitchen."

I heard him chuckle, deep and rumbling, as he walked away. I covered my eyes with one arm as I stretched out on the couch.

As I lay there and he rustled around in the kitchen, my mind wandered to his life.

Where had he been all these years? What had he been doing? Had he had other relationships? His phone number didn't have the same area code as people in our hometown so did he even live there? If not, where the heck did he live?

At the sound of the washer lid closing, I scrambled into a sitting position, not wanting to give him the opportunity to catch me lying down. The way he had my body humming for him when I stood, I could only imagine what he'd do to me if he got me onto my back. Stefan rounded the corner and came straight toward me.

Being his usual predictable self, he took a seat right next to me and placed his arm along the back of the sofa. The semi-naughty grin on his face made my stomach flip and I crossed my arms over my chest defensively.

And, because I wasn't wearing a bra. I knew he'd stare at my chest if given half a chance.

"Whaddya want?"

He repositioned himself slightly, making sure his body was aimed toward me, as he answered. "I wanna have sex."

"What?" Screeching, I stood up. "No!"

He grabbed my hands firmly in his, pulling me back down to the seat as I studied his face. Not smiling and not frowning. My stomach dropped as I realized that he was serious.

"Listen to me, Ellie," He requested softly. I stilled as he lifted his hand to push a piece of stray hair behind my ear. "We obviously still desire each other."

I snickered at this. "Do we? What in the world makes you think I still want you?"

Not rising to the bait, he smiled and cupped my face in his hand. "I had you in my arms just last week. Your body betrayed you. I don't know why you are fighting the truth so hard. Let's see if that was a one time thing or if the spark truly is as strong as my need for you."

I didn't know whether to be excited at his words or insulted. "You just want my body then, is that it? You traveled all the way here to have sex with me?"

He leaned closer, pressing a kiss to my jaw. I tamped down a shiver of arousal as he lingered, caressing my cheek slowly with his thumb. The touch of his hand on my leg and the heat it emitted soaked through the soft fabric of my pajama pants, marking me.

"I want more than that, Ellie, but I am willing to take what you will give me," he murmured with another kiss to the jaw as his lips traveled in the direction of my mouth. "If, right now, it's one night of lusty and passionate sex with the hottest chick I've ever known, then I will take it."

I could argue with that.

I should argue with his reasoning. But I didn't want to. The hottest chick he'd ever known? Really?

He didn't say anything more as he kept kissing me and caressing my cheek with one hand, while stroking my leg with the other.

"You...you don't have anybody else?"

Freezing in place, he dragged his eyes to mine. "Would I be here if I did?"

How was I to answer that? It had been a long time, I didn't know this man. Stefan from five years ago didn't equal Stefan today...did it?

"I don't know, would you?"

His blue eyes darkened, deepening to near black as he brought his other hand up to my face and cupped it, holding me still.

"Do you have somebody else Ellie? If you do, tell me now and I'll walk away."

I didn't. I'd only dated one other person in all these years and that was just last year, after years of therapy. Knowing I needed to answer his question, I shook my head.

"When is the last time we made love, honey?"

I knew he was aroused, holding me in place as he was. He'd always been in charge in the bedroom and I loved it. I couldn't look away.

The question, however, made my chest tighten with anxiety. I licked my lips and his eyes dropped down, his grip tightening as if he was on the verge of losing control and trying to hold off. I wanted to scream 'kiss me!' so I wouldn't have to answer any more questions.

"Before you left to go abroad."

Yeah, he'd stuck around almost a complete year after returning from his trip. There had been no hiding the fact I'd been attacked as it had been in the news and he took me not wanting to be touched as just me being skittish. I'd fallen deeper and deeper into my depression and our relationship had ended with a gigantic explosion of frustration - sexual and otherwise.

"That's right." His eyes were blazing now. "It's been six years and I still get aroused just thinking of you. Not even naked, just thinking of *you* Ellie. So, what am I supposed to do? Just go through life wanting you and being unable to have you? I can't do that."

Staring right back at him, I wondered how much he remembered.

Did he realize that he was touching me more now than I had let him since he'd returned from his trip? Did he recall how I would shy away from his touch and wince if he came up behind me unexpectedly? Had he never really considered why else I wouldn't let him touch me?

I should've told him the truth that instant. Told him the secret I'd been - and still was - so ashamed of even though it hadn't been my fault. Yet as he sat so close I could almost feel him breathing, completely focused on me, the words wouldn't come.

I wanted him. I didn't really see a reason to deny him or myself what we both desired.

Lying about how much I longed for his touch seemed ridiculous, especially when he knew. He read me like a book and I let him, because it gave me an excuse to give in. To have what I wanted without admitting it out loud.

And even though I knew that any attempt at a relationship would end up going down in flames, the question remaining was a simple one.

I just hoped I didn't regret it.

"Only one night?"

# CHAPTER SIX

At my reply, Stefan stood up and swooped me into his arms, using one arm to support my backside as I wrapped my legs around him.

"Which way to your bedroom?"

"Uh..." Never imagining that this would happen, I closed my eyes and sucked in a breath. Pointing toward the general direction of my bedroom, he chuckled.

"I'm sure it can't be hard to find," he declared as he carried me down the hall.

My own need shocked me. Living so far away for so many years had numbed the memories of our life together. I'd built a life in another city, got the help I'd desperately needed and had come out relatively unscathed considering.

It wasn't that I hadn't wondered through the years about what had become of him. I had but I'd also distanced myself from the feelings and buried them deep down. Apparently, I hadn't buried them deep enough. I'd agreed to sex even though I knew the idea had the potential to backfire in my face. And he carried me in his arms, giving me a sense of fulfillment I hadn't felt since before the attack.

Having reached the bedroom, I noticed only a sliver of light from the street lamps outside coming through the crack in the curtains. Dusk had fallen, leaving my room dancing with shadows. Stefan didn't turn on the light. Laying me in the center of the bed, he eased down beside me and pulled me into his arms.

He'd never bothered to put another shirt on, so I rested my head against his bare chest. The light smattering of hair on his chest caught me by surprise. It used to be thicker, although not unbearably so. Tilting my head toward his head, I could only make out his chin.

"Please tell me you do *not* man-scape!"

"Okay, I don't man-scape," he whispered. Laughing, he slipped his hands under my tank and pushed it up. "Take it off."

He released me just enough for me to yank it over my head. A moment later, I lay on my back as he hovered over me, my heart thundering in my chest. Feeling as if it were going to burst if he didn't kiss me, I wrapped my arms around his neck and yanked his mouth down to mine.

The wild swirling in my stomach at the touch of his lips against mine made me not want to think. I just wanted to feel. Feel the heat of his body against mine, his hands moving over every inch of my body, the passion for me he'd declared so openly. Mostly, I wanted to feel what I felt with him before.

Safe. Loved. Free.

He lifted his mouth off mine, moving positions to get more comfortable even as he covered one breast with a palm. Leaning down, his mouth covered the nipple and lightly bit it, instantly making me moan.

His hand traced lightly over my skin, down to my stomach and back up, building anticipation. Then, on another trip down, it stopped at the waist of my pajama bottoms and stilled. He nipped me again before lifting his head.

"Did you miss me?" I could hear the need in his voice, roughened with desire. "Did you miss this, Ellie?"

"Yes," I breathed, gasping as he slipped past my waistband at the answer. My mind muddled, I didn't know which question I referred to and I didn't care. I just wanted - no, *needed* - him to touch me. "More than you know."

Climbing back on top of me with just the support of one arm, he hissed. "I've been waiting to hear that for a long time. Look at me."

I looked up into his eyes as his hand slipped further, cupping me gently. I shifted my legs, surging up to try and get his hand to move but it stayed still.

"Tell me your secret Ellie. And you can have what you want."

I couldn't even be pleased at the revelation that the answers he'd spoken of when he'd first arrived included my secret. I didn't want to talk about this, I wanted sex, dammit!

I moved my hips again, knowing the movement excited him.

"Bastard," I spat and he lifted his body away even as he kept his hand in place. His finger lightly stroked me now, sending tingles to all the right places. "I won't play this game with you."

Parting me gently, he chuckled. "Oh you will."

I didn't like his arrogant attitude as he continued to explore with the finger and entered just enough to tease.

"Damn you!" I jerked my lower body up and toward him, succeeding in making the digit impale me deeper. I crowed with the victory. "Ah-ha!"

He surged forward and I cried out a mere second before he recaptured my lips, punishing me and my stubbornness with them. Tracing my lips with his tongue, he shoved another finger inside me. As I gasped with delighted shock at his roughness, he thrust his tongue into my mouth and dueled with mine. Again, I tasted mint on his breath and wondered how he always managed to have such fresh breath.

When he removed his hand, I moaned into his mouth and he laughed. Our tongues continued to wage war with one another as his hand drifted up my side, his blunt nails scratching ever so lightly on their trail. His other hand caught in my hair and held on as his wandering hand trailed down again and slipped my bottoms down, exposing my legs to the air.

Releasing my lips, he showered kisses all over my face before nibbling the tip of my ear, then whispered, "I always did love your hair. It's not as long as it used to be, but it's still long enough that I can grab and hold on to it."

I smiled. It had been down to my hips the last time he had seen me but when I had moved, I'd chopped it all off. Now I kept it just above my shoulders, a cut I found much easier to take care of. As for him holding on to it...that had always been one of my favorite things, but I said nothing and brought my hands up to his shoulders.

Considering how passionate he'd been in the living room, his restraint surprised me. Gently kicking off my bottoms as his lips explored my neck, I lay there in nothing but my undies and had never felt so naked. We'd had sex before but this time, it felt different. I couldn't place my reaction in any rational category. Maybe it was because we weren't together; we were just two people who used to date and still wanted to have sex with the other. Or maybe, it's because I knew he planned to make love to me and I wasn't sure my feelings were on par with his.

Either way, I decided to stop over-thinking this moment and just enjoy it.

I slid my hands down his arms and back up, before moving up to his neck and into his hair. I loved the color - a shade of red so deep, it looked brown when wet - and always had. Cropped short, the small tickling sensation as I ran my hand across the tip of the haircut amused me, as usual.

"Ah!"

He'd nipped my neck and at my surprise, he pulled away. I studied him as he stared at me, the lack of light in the room making it near impossible to see much. He rolled off me and I leaned up on my elbows, deciding to take control of the situation. Impatient at the speed things were going, I rested my hand on his arm.

"You should take off your pants," I suggested and he looked over at me, his eyes widened with amazement, no doubt at my boldness.

When he didn't move, I sat up and got onto my knees, making sure he watched as I lowered my panties. I didn't think his eyes could get any wider but he just lay there, mouth agape.

Suddenly, I felt self-conscious and vulnerable. I was lost. We used to play around when together before and sometimes, I'd be in charge, but he always loved to tell me what to do anyway. I had loved it; hell I still loved it. I figured offering myself on a platter would rock his world.

Yet he just sat there, staring. I gulped, afraid I'd made a big mistake.

Stumbling over my words, I rolled toward the edge of the bed and sat up. "I-I don't think this is such a good idea."

"Wait."

The command stopped me in my tracks, but I could no longer see him. It was silent for mere moments before I heard the zipper on his jeans. My heart stuttered, beating rapidly in my chest as he continued to undress. I didn't dare move, waiting in anticipation for whatever came next.

Then, a firm touch on my shoulder as he came up behind me. Slowly wrapping his arms around my waist, the heat from his body chased away the sudden chill I'd gained in my fear of being rejected. His breath upon my neck thrilled as much as his touch. Our closeness aroused me to the point of pain and I wanted to turn in his arms, but I didn't. I waited for him to speak and he didn't disappoint.

"Don't ever leave me tease me like that and then think you can just walk away," he growled, grabbing my hair and tilting my head back toward him. "Shouldn't you know by now that there is nothing you can do that will turn me off?"

"B-but I thought you—"

"You're wrong," he interjected with a chuckle. "You surprised me is all. We really need to work on your thoughts of what is surprise and what is rejection, Ellie."

His other arm tightened around my middle and pulled me toward him. Placing me on my back in the center of the bed, he gently spread my legs. His hard body above mine once again, I cradled his nakedness with mine.

"You sure you don't wanna play anymore?" His hand slipped between both of us and found me once more. Teasing me, taunting me enough that the answer to his question became lost in the surge of sensation.

I whimpered, the sound escaping against my will as he used two fingers to penetrate me again.

"God, you're so wet," he groaned, speeding up while using his thumb to stroke and give me pleasure on the outside. "You always were a hot little sex machine."

I laughed. The raw desire in his voice also had tears prickling in my eyes.

Why had I ever let him get away? After all I'd done, even if he didn't know, he was the one person who could get me hot in two seconds with just a look, a touch, a kiss. I'd been such a fool to push him away, but my pride wouldn't let me admit it out loud.

I wanted this moment, this chance to be close. To feel a connection, passion, and maybe even hope that things between us would be okay. The anxiety in my throat wouldn't let me examine my feelings any closer. Reaching down between us, I wrapped my hand around him.

"Oh god," he hissed, closing his eyes with a moan. "You're a naughty one."

There was no need for me to reply. I reveled in the power I had in that moment, a control I relished having and one I loved to wield. Especially with Stefan. The sounds coming from him had my heart singing. I never thought I'd hear it again and yet here we were once more.

I needed him.

"Please," I gasped as his fingers went deep again and my body clenched around them. "I don't wanna wait anymore."

The sound of him gritting his teeth had me smiling.

"You still take birth control?"

"Yeah, I do. Pill."

Not that it had saved me when I had needed it to the most. I had, however, changed the kind I used a long time ago.

"Do you want...are you still...?"

Surprised that he remembered, I laughed. "Ha, yeah, most foreign objects still cause me to break out." I was -and always had been - allergic to latex and spermicides, among other things. I hated it but that's the way it always had been.

"I guess that rules out food play still."

His words might have amused me had I not been so turned on I wanted to scream with frustration.

With a sigh, I wiggled, impatient. "Are we done talking now?"

"It's your show, Ellie," he teased me as he slowly removed his fingers. "Take me and put me into you, honey."

*Yes!* I put a hand on his neck, pulling his lips down to meet mine even as I guided his arousal to me. The instant our bodies touched, he surged in one smooth motion. Our moans of pleasure were almost synchronized, swallowed up in our deep kissing.

Wrapping my legs around him, we became as close as two people could be. My nipples brushed against his chest, perking up instantly, almost painfully. He moved slowly, pulling almost to the edge before sinking deep again. I knew my nails were digging into his back but he didn't seem to care. Our mouths were still fused and he moved a hand down to my ass, squeezing it with one hand as his rhythm sped up.

Sex between us remained everything I remembered and at the same time, became more than I could have imagined. Our bodies moved together as if they had never been apart, falling into a familiar rhythm I'd never forget for as long as I lived.

Stefan released my mouth and trailed kisses along my jaw and down to my neck. His other hand wrapped in my hair and as he brought his lips close to mine, he held my head still.

"Talk to me," he demanded. "Tell me what you need right now."

"Touch me. I need you to touch me."

His hand snaked between us. So close to the edge, I could feel my release building, as the sweet pleasure radiated down my legs. Stefan's movements were shallow now, faster. I tensed up as my mind blanked, focusing on the sensations he urged my body to feel.

Responses my body hadn't been inclined to offer in so long and especially not with the only person I'd had sex with since then.

He must have seen my eyes squeezed shut because he brought his lips to mine and breathed, "Relax and let go, honey."

The words, uttered in his deep sexy voice, pushed me over the edge. My release had me gasping, stronger than even the one I'd had in that room upstairs back at his mother's house. It took me a moment to realize the sobs I heard were my own.

Stefan pulled his hand away even as he stiffened, releasing my hair and wrapping his arms around me. I heard him groan into my shoulder as he stroked deep one final time and stopped, shuddering.

"Oh god," I cried. "What have we done?"

# CHAPTER SEVEN

Rolling off me, Stefan cradled me in his arms and I hid my face in his chest as I cried.

The flood of emotions had caught me off guard. The feeling of him in my arms, in *me*, when I thought we'd never even speak again had touched a part of me I had long ago locked away.

At the stroke of his hand on my hair, I sobbed harder.

"Shhh, Ellie. It'll be all right," he soothed. "Don't cry, honey."

Pushing away from him, he let me go. Lying back on the pillows, he looked at ease, peaceful. And here I lay, a jumble of anxieties and confusion, crying my heart out. So I took it out on him, snapping.

"How many times do I have to tell you that I'm not your honey!"

Exiting the bed as quickly as possible, I stormed down the hall and into my bathroom, slamming the door behind me. Locking it, I stood in front of the mirror and placed my hands on the sink, lowering my head as I tried to call myself down.

Less than a minute had passed before he knocked lightly on the door.

"Ellie…please come out and talk to me."

I hated the polite tone of voice, almost consoling. Like he cared about me.

*He does care,* my heart chided me. *Nobody travels across the country to their ex-love for one night of sex.*

Right.

I found it hard to convince myself that he cared about me. I had pushed him away, but he'd also walked without fighting back. What's to say he wouldn't do it again after he got tired of me this time around? Nothing, that's what.

I felt silly standing there, looking into the mirror at the red and swollen dark brown eyes of a woman who had just had what probably qualified as the most amazing sex she'd ever had. In that second, I hated myself and I hated the insecurities that kept me from storming out there to tell him all my secrets and all my pain.

Jumping in front of a train wasn't a smart idea and I had to keep reminding myself of that. Giving Stefan what he wanted and opening myself up like that would be like asking a power larger than myself to run over me. I would have to be insane to even consider such a thing.

In truth, I didn't think he'd understand. I didn't think anybody would ever understand. Only Liliana had and - barring her ex-husband - she'd taken my secret to the grave with her, even if she had threatened otherwise. I wondered if she knew that once Stefan saw me again, he'd be unwilling to let me go again. Perhaps that had been her plan all along - to say she'd tell, knowing he'd be nearby and unable to resist the lure of a secret, the thrill of chasing me.

"Stop running from me Ellie. I only want what is best for you," he pleaded through the door. "Whatever it is, we can work through it."

Damn it, why did he have to be so freaking perfect?

He'd use that line before, all those years ago and I'd doubted him. I didn't believe he meant it. I considered my secret dark and him, the epitome of everything light. Funny, smart and kind he could no doubt have anybody he desired. Always gainfully employed and someone that everybody liked. How could he even begin to understand the pain I'd went through?

He should've been married with kids by now, instead of practically obsessing over me. What had I done to deserve such devotion? Nothing in my mind.

*Now I just feel as if I've prevented him from moving on with his life. Great!*

Dabbing my eyes dry, I walked to the door and unlocked it, swinging the door open.

He stumbled back from the door before catching his footing and crossed his arms. The action brought my eyes to his chest, only to emphasize the fact he hadn't bothered to put any clothing on yet. Still feeling vulnerable, I reached behind the door and grabbed the robe, using it to cover up physically even though it couldn't hide the emotional impact of our coupling just moments ago.

"I'm going to bed," I announced. "I have to work in the morning."

Even he nodded, he approached me with a smile. "I know. I'll just finish settling in tomorrow while you're at work."

I took a step back even as my hands itched to touch him. "How can you even afford to be away from work?"

He laughed, the sound deep and sexy.

Sexy? God, I had it bad.

"I brought my work with me. It's all on this nifty device we call a laptop," he joked.

I hated how...*happy* he seemed. Next to the way I felt - emotionally destroyed was an apt description - his cheerfulness only made me angrier. The sex had completely destroyed my illusions of there being no spark anymore.

He felt it and knew our attraction hadn't waned at all.

A fool to believe otherwise, that's what I was.

"Night," I said curtly, turning on my heel and heading toward the bedroom.

"Night honey!" He replied with a chuckle.

Gritting my teeth at his endearment, I slammed the door shut.

The immense feeling of satisfaction at the sound didn't last as long as I thought it would.

As I climbed into bed, I hoped now that he was here in person, he'd stop haunting my dreams.

~*~

The morning came before I wanted it to as my alarm blared from the top of my dresser.

I groaned.

Why had I decided that putting it across the room was a good idea?

Oh right, because it was supposed to get me out of bed. And it worked, since getting up was to get the thing to stop with the incessant beeping.

Throwing back the covers, I stumbled out of bed and over to the alarm, shutting it off with the button on the side. Throwing my robe on, I walked out to the living room, only to find no Stefan on my couch.

*What the hell? Where had he gone?*

Continuing into the kitchen, his luggage sitting by the washer confirmed that he was still here and left me utterly confused. It was just hitting six-thirty in the morning, where could he have gone to this early?

Then again, I didn't need to care about what he was doing. At least he wasn't here bothering me.

Filling up and turning on the electric kettle to make myself some tea, I was head deep in a cupboard looking for my frying pan when I heard the door slam.

Not expecting the noise, I brought my head up, only to hit it on the rim of the cupboard frame. "Son of a bitch!"

"Uh, Ellie? Are you okay?"

Standing up, I rubbed the back of my head as he came into view and stopped just inside the kitchen entryway.

I never thought it could happen to me, but the sight of him left me speechless.

He wore workout clothes - a tight gray shirt with matching shorts - that left his incredibly muscled legs bared. Gulping, I traveled the length of his body back up to his face, where I found him grinning at me      .
His face glistened with sweat from this distance and I

instantly knew what he'd been doing - out running at an hour I wouldn't be caught awake at to save my life.

"Oh yeah, I always have men coming into my place at six-thirty in the morning and shocking the crap out of me."

"How was I supposed to know you would have your head somewhere dangerous this early?" He retorted, the smile never leaving his face as he walked toward me. "Let me look."

"Ugh, no!" Putting a hand out to stop his approach, I grimaced. "I need to hurry up and shower. I have to leave for work soon."

He stopped his advance on me and leaned against the counter. "Do you want me to make you some breakfast?"

Again, I wondered who this man was as I shook my head. "No thanks. I don't eat in the morning."

"Tsk, tsk. That's not healthy at all," he chided me as I walked past.

"Gee, thanks for telling me that *honey*," I mocked, entering the bathroom.

The sound of him as he busted out laughing was the last thing I heard as the door closed.

I locked it for safe measure, just in case he had any ideas to join me in the shower. Though, if he did want to, Stefan could no doubt find a way to get inside. He had always been quite resourceful when we were younger.

~*~

After I'd finished showering, I opened the door to go to my room, and heard Stefan speaking to somebody.

Pausing for a second while trying to keep from eavesdropping, I peeked around the corner anyway. He faced away from me while talking into his cell phone, staring out the living room window.

"I only planned to take a week off work, so I should be back in six days." He paused, presumably to listen, running a hand over his head. "I know, but I'll be home soon."

My curiosity knew no bounds. Who the hell was he talking to? Six days and he'd be gone? What was he hoping to accomplish in that time? Although, look what he had managed to do in less than twenty-four hours!

Attempting to tip toe to my room so I could keep listening, the floor creaked beneath my foot and I winced. Looking over my shoulder, I discovered that he'd turned around, staring at me with a less than amused look on his face.

"I gotta go," he said into the phone even as continued to scowl at me. "I'll call you later okay?"

I took off toward my room, but not before hearing him say 'me too' and hanging up.

He walked into the bedroom as I was zipping up a black pencil skirt. Ignoring him, I picked out a cream silk blouse and buttoned it up, all while he stood behind me with his arms over his chest.

"Do you always listen in on other people's conversations, Ellie?"

Rolling my eyes at him in the mirror, I searched through my jewelry box and chose a pair of pearl earrings my mother had given me years before as a gift. As I fastened them in my ears, I flashed him a smile. "I didn't intend to. I was trying not to interrupt."

He quirked a brow and scowled deeper, as if he doubted my sincerity.

I also didn't know why I was being nice in the face of his blatant distrust in regards to me. "I am curious about who you were talking to, I'll admit that."

Finished with dressing, I turned around as he replied. "If you were my girlfriend, I might think it was information you needed, maybe even deserved to know. But you're not."

Well, he was in a mood today. Two could play that game.

"Ah well, I'll live without knowing then," I quipped. "I need to leave for work now."

Intending to walk past him to grab my things and put my heels on, he caught my arm in one hand.

"Please consider coming back with me. You know, back home. You even have your own place there now."

Yanking my arm away, I laughed as I left the room.

"You've got to be kidding! I told you, I have a life here."

He walked out of the room as I finally got my shoes on and slung my purse over my shoulder.

"Ellie..." If he wasn't such a self-assured jackass, I might believe I heard a bit of pleading in his voice as he said my name. "You've been gone too long. It's time to come home."

"This *is* my home," I emphasized. "But if you wanna go back there now, go for it. Me, I'm gonna be late if I don't leave this instant. Feel free to eat whatever though. There is a ton of food in the fridge."

He said nothing else as I opened the door and walked through, shutting it quietly behind me.

# CHAPTER EIGHT

The moment I sat down at my desk, my boss buzzed me. "Elizabeth, would you come into my office please?"

Something in his tone of voice had my stomach clenching with anxiety.

Not bothering to respond to him, I rose to my feet on uncertain legs and walked slowly toward the door. Taking a deep breath, I opened it and walked in, choosing to just stand in the doorway until I was further instructed.

It didn't take long.

"Please, close the door and have a seat. Would you like a drink?"

I shook my head and closed the door quietly, before walking deeper into the room and sitting down.

Nolan Reynolds was the nicest man I had ever met. Taking me in fresh out of college five years before, he'd given a chance to a Business student from the middle of nowhere. To be fair, I'd had a four-point-oh GPA and an activity filled resume. Even though I'd had horrible depression my final year, school was something I'd worked hard at and wasn't going to let that go up in flames as my relationship with Stefan had. Getting a job across the country just when I'd needed it had been perfect.

Right now, Nolan was watching me with sad eyes and I knew this visit wasn't a good one.

"The company is downsizing," he began and unable to handle the sudden empathy in his face, I looked away, desperate to see anything but his sad gaze. My eyes finally settled on my hands. "I'm afraid that although I tried to save your job, the board said we have to give preference to those with seniority and unfortunately, that list is long. There aren't enough spots for me to keep you on."

There it was. I couldn't believe I was being let go.

As tears pricked at my eyes and slowly spilled down my cheeks, I sniffled. I heard rather than saw Nolan pull a tissue out of the box and lean over his desk, crumpling some papers beneath his body.

"Here, Elizabeth," he said softly, hanging the tissue in my face. "I'm so sorry. I truly argued with them for hours about it."

Grabbing it, I wiped my face and made sure I was okay before looking up. He had sat back down and was just watching me, hands clasped on top of his desk.

"Well, thanks for breaking it to me in private."

He nodded. "They just brought down the final decision this morning. I was hoping they'd change their mind last minute but they said anyone who is being let go needs to be gone by Friday. I figured it a kindness to tell you sooner rather than later."

"I will clean out my desk then. Thanks Nolan," I murmured, standing up.

As I turned to walk away, he spoke. "Do you know where you'll go?"

With a humorless laugh, I threw my hands up in the air, glancing over my shoulder at him. "Wouldn't you know, as luck would have it, I just inherited a house last week. In my hometown."

His wince at that told me he knew exactly whose house I had inherited.

"Just...," he coughed. "Feel free to put me down as a reference. You were an excellent employee and I will help you try to get any job you desire. Whoever hires you will be one lucky s.o.b."

Throwing a watery smile his way, I nodded. "Thanks. I will do that."

With that, I walked out to my desk and starting placing the very few things I had there into my purse.

As I headed to the elevator, I really had no desire to go back to my apartment. Stefan would know instantly that I'd lost my job and then his harping for me to go home would never cease. Not that I wasn't seriously considering it right now.

After all, I didn't have many ties to this area. I had never been much of a social person - especially after that night so long ago - which made the job here most of my adult interaction. There had been an occasional late night where we'd order food and chat while working on projects. As Nolan's executive assistant, I'd attended most meetings with him and we had become really close. I had taken him at his word that he'd fought for me but I also knew how business ran. He might have an important position here, yet when it came to hiring and firing, that meant nothing compared to the Board of Director's decisions.

I had never gotten close to anyone though. The only person I'd dated in all these years I had met in my therapist's office. She hadn't been happy but we both avoided talking about the other during sessions. I hadn't really wanted to discuss him anyway - I'd been there to work out other things. Once the relationship had ended, I'd stopped going to therapy and right now, I really regretted that. I could use someone to talk to.

So as I stepped off the elevator and exited the building, Pulling out my cell phone, I searched through the contacts until I found the person I was looking for. Someone who had never let me down and that I knew I could count on to give me some good advice.

Grace.

~*~

Grace sounded breathless as she picked up the phone.

"Hello?"

Then I remembered she still only had a house phone, which she had probably run to from across the house.

"Grace, it's Elizabeth."

"Oh! Hey!" Her voice instantly perked up. "How are you doing?"

"Besides just losing my job, I'm fucking terrific!" My voice broke.

"Wow, sorry to hear that. What will you do?"

I sighed into the phone. "Honestly, I have no idea! I've not got much keeping me here honestly. The good news is that I've still got three weeks of this month to move out if I decide to do that. I'll have to eat my deposit with the lack of notice, though."

"Are...are you coming back home?" Her voice had gone quiet.

"I might," I admitted. "After all, I am the proud owner of Liliana's house now."

"Yeah..."

When she didn't say anything else, I changed the subject as I climbed into my car.

"How is Lyndsey?"

I was asking about her daughter. I'd seen a picture here and there, along with our random Skype chats. She had green eyes and was the spitting image of her mother, except for her strawberry blond hair. Grace had found out she was pregnant just three months after I'd left town, which had shocked me but she told me it was the result of a one night stand. The father was a scumbag who apparently didn't see his daughter and Grace refused to even talk about what would happen when Lyndsey got curious one day.

"She's great! She'll turn four in just five weeks, I can't believe it!"

"I can't either." And really, I couldn't. Time seemed to have flown by and for the first time in years, I'd realized how much time had passed. It was like waking up after a very vivid dream that had seemed so real, but wasn't. That was my life here, and now I was going to have to deal with all the feelings I'd buried, and the people I'd hurt when I'd left behind.

I wasn't sure I could make it up to Stefan, nor was I convinced a second attempt at our relationship would work. With Liliana gone, I was glad I'd gotten to see her even if it had brought the memories rushing back with a vengeance. And my mother...I wasn't looking forward to facing all our problems head on. Yet, right now, I knew that it was the decent thing to do.

"I suppose by then I'll be in town. Are you throwing a birthday party for her?"

"Yeah! Mostly friends and family, but of course, you are welcome to come!"

She was back to her perky attitude again so I decided to leave out the fact that Stefan was visiting me. I'm sure I'd hear a long spiel about how I needed to move on. She'd never liked him after he'd walked away, even though she hadn't understood my depression. I'd spent the rest of that summer with Liliana and Grace had never known the truth either.

But she'd never walked away like Stefan had. Instead, I'd been the one who had left town and gotten a job far away.

"Great. I'll let you know what I decide. I gotta drive home now."

"Okay! Lyndsey is calling for me anyway! Talk later!"

Hanging up, I sat in my car for a few more minutes as I contemplated my options.

Losing my job was truly unexpected but I wasn't surprised for some reason. I'd know that one day, my past would catch up with me and I'd have no choice but to deal with it. True, I didn't have to go all the way across the country to my hometown. I could stay here and job hunt as I had enough in savings to last a year or more if I cut back just a bit.

Then again, that also meant I could go back and settle in, see if I truly wanted to stay there without needing to find work. Patch things up with my mother, which would involve divulging those long ago summer months when all I'd wanted to do was crawl into a hole and die. Aside from Liliana, the only blessing at the time had been the fact I had no recollection of the sexual assault - and I still didn't. I couldn't imagine what it would be like to remember and I stayed grateful for that small boon.

Either way, as I put my car into gear and drove out of the parking garage, I knew that only one thing mattered.

I had to do this for myself and myself only.

My head clearer, I prepared for the onslaught of feelings I knew I'd experience once I was in Stefan's presence again and he knew I was going home.

# CHAPTER NINE

Stefan was sitting at the table when I arrived home, tapping away at the keys on his laptop. He looked up at me with wide eyes and then at his watch. His brows drew down in apparent confusion.

"Isn't it a bit early for you to be home? You just left barely two hours ago."

Gritting my teeth, I dropped my purse on the table and leaned down to take off my heels.

"Really?" I dropped my mouth open as I straightened, bringing my eyes to meet his. "I guess my clock at work must be broken! I thought it was the end of the work day."

His lips quirked up at the corners. "No joke. I'd have to reconsider working for a company with a broken clock."

Dropping into the chair across from me, I tilted my head to the side as I studied him without responding.

He was looking at me, yet his fingers tapped at the keys as if I wasn't even in the room. At some point in the last couple of hours he had showered and changed clothing. In a pair of khaki trousers and an unbuttoned white cambric shirt that bared his not-one-ounce-of-fat chest, he looked yummy enough to eat. His relaxed pose was at odds with the concentration on his face when I'd first walked in.

"What are you typing?" I was impressed by his typing skills, but only because I wished I could type that fast without looking at the keys or screen.

"Typing up an email. One sec," he winked at me and clicked on his mouse. "There. All done. Now, where were we?"

Pushing away from the table, he turned the chair toward me and focused his eyes on me.

I bit my lip, looking away.

"Well..." I swallowed, unsure of how to continue. "They...um...well, I got laid off."

When he didn't instantly start cheering, I faced him, only to find him staring at me with a look of complete surprise on his face.

"What, no smug satisfaction that I have no job and therefore, no need to stay here?"

The flash of hurt on his face was so fast I nearly missed it. I almost felt guilty, considering our interlude the evening before.

Until he spoke. "Oh goodie, just what I always wanted," he drawled with obvious sarcasm. "You comin' home because you lost your job instead of by your own choice."

Standing abruptly, I strolled closer to him until our knees touched and put my hands on the arms of his chair, leaning in so our noses nearly touched. I nearly laughed at his sudden intake of breath at my proximity to him.

"Make no mistake, Stefan. I *am* coming home by choice because I have more than enough money to stay here and look for another job for at least a year, if not more." I really didn't know how much money I had, which meant it was time I called my Accountant but that didn't matter right this second.

His eyebrows shot up at that even though he didn't say anything. His eyes dropped to my chest though, which is when I realized he could see down my shirt. Ignoring that fact, I continued.

"Let's also be clear that I am coming home *because I want to* and not because of you or anything you've done or said."

Then, he grinned and the naughty look in his eyes that accompanied it sent my pulse racing.

Before I could move, I was straddling his lap and his right hand was sliding under my skirt. Wrapping his other hand in my hair, he tugged my head down and captured my lips with his, both of our eyes closing upon the contact. Tracing the entrance to my mouth with his tongue, I decided to go with it for the moment and gave myself freely. Sighing, I parted my lips and his tongue plunged inside, instantly sparring with mine.

His hand had reached the apex of my thighs. I tasted his growl of frustration as he tried to cup me in his hand, only to be thwarted by the tightness of the skirt. Releasing my hair and pulling his other hand out, we continued to devour each others mouths as he pushed the skirt up on each side. Another growl as the fabric stopped moving at the tightest part and his hands found the zipper in the back, quickly loosening the garment and shoving it up onto my waist.

Then, he moved to my blouse. Making quick work of the buttons, he shoved it open and encircled my body with his arms, cradling my ass with one hand and supporting my back with the other.

"When I stand up, wrap your legs around me," he murmured into my mouth just seconds before he stood.

Doing as he bid, he started walking, only to shock me as I felt the wall against my back.

"What...why don't we go to the bedroom?" I asked as I ripped my lips away from him.

Drawing his head back, he reached a hand between us as he answered with hooded eyes.

"Because I want to fuck you against this wall."

And with those words, the fire that had been building in me lit up completely. The rush of desire almost had me gasping. He hadn't even really touched me and I knew I was ready for him. And at this point, I didn't have a good reason not to reach out and take this moment for me.

Yet, I knew I had to make something clear.

"Hold on," I implored, putting one hand to his chest even as I felt him undo the button on his pants.

He just stood there, staring at me in silence, waiting.

"This...whatever it is. Between us. It's for the rest of the time you're here and that's it."

At that, his eyes darkened and I thought he would argue. Instead, he shrugged and I felt vaguely disappointed.

"If that's what you want," he declared.

Before I could say yes, that's what I wanted, he claimed my lips with his own again, the kiss more punishing this time in its ferocity. He stepped closer and I felt his hand push my flimsy thong to the side. Preparing for the onslaught I knew was coming, I brought arms up and around his neck, anchoring my body to his.

One, two fingers found me and I moaned as he rocked them in and out, over and over until I thought I'd go mad. The faster his hands went, the more I moaned. Ripping his mouth from mine, he nibbled my earlobe before searing a path down my neck, the kisses hot against my skin. I knew they weren't marking me but it felt that way.

Tilting my head slightly to give him better access, I buried my face in his neck, kissing the exposed skin there and tasting his salty skin. So focused on the sensations, I jumped at the sound of his voice, so deep with desire my insides clenched at the sound.

"Your body is so ready for me. Are you ready?" The words were just above a whisper, the self-control he was exhibiting apparent in the stillness of his body.

"Mmmhmm," was my reply and that was all he needed.

Lining up our bodies, he slowly entered me. The bite of his teeth against my neck was nothing compared to the torture below, the center of me that was nearly begging for release. When he grabbed my hips and shoved me all the way down, I screamed as my orgasm rolled over me but Stefan didn't slow down.

Over and over, he pulled to the edge before slamming me down again, at a pace that had me gasping for breath. The raw act of possession left me captivated, and my body on the edge of another orgasm. Then, he whispered in my ear, slowing to an almost glacial pace.

"Tell me you're mine."

I froze, even as the rest of me was on fire, begging for relief. "No."

He retreated, leaving our bodies barely connected and me gripping his shoulders. "Now Ellie. Say it. You're mine. You always have been, just admit it and I'll give you what you want."

He surged forward again and I sobbed as he left just as quickly.

"No, damn you!"

"Fucking say it! I love you dammit, the least you can do is admit that you're mine as much as I am yours."

My body quivering with need, I could no longer deny him - or myself.

"Fine! I'm yours!" I shouted. "I'm yours, I've always fucking been yours."

And with that, he pounded into me. Again and again.

I shattered into a million pieces as he grunted, trembling as his body shook with its own release.

Through my tears, I whispered, "Sometimes, I really don't like you."

Bringing his eyes up to mine, I saw the pain in them as he pressed a soft kiss to my lips.

"That's okay honey. At times, I don't really like you either."

~*~

"Did you know?"

It was near midnight and we were lying in my bed, naked. I didn't figure there was any need to continue making him sleep on the couch - and admittedly, I liked being held. It was different than it used to be in a delicious sort of way. He was more muscled now and the weight of his body against mine as we spooned made me feel safe. Odd, since at this point, I considered him the biggest threat to the little bubble of a life I'd created for myself.

"Hmm? Did I know what?" He whispered as his arm caressed my side, dipping down into my waist before rising at the curve of my hips.

I knew this to be a soothing gesture of his and smiled at the sameness of some things even among changes.

"That your mother was going to give me the house. I mean, before she asked you all to sign off on it."

"Yeah, of course. Since I was the firstborn, she'd always said I'd be the one to get it, so she and I had a long talk beforehand."

I tensed up. "Wait...you were supposed to get the house?"

I turned my head as if to look at him, but he had me locked in his embrace with the other arm so I couldn't really turn around to face him.

"Yep," was all he said as I felt his smile against my neck.

"Why would you let her give it to me? Neither of you even knew if I was still alive."

He laughed then. "Of course we knew you were alive! We may not have known where you lived, but your mother constantly assured my mother that you were all right. I have to give your mom credit though - for someone who is a major gossip, she never once let it slip where you were living at."

That was pretty good. I can't say I ever bothered to ask and it's not like anybody had ever shown up here. He still hadn't answered my question though.

"And...?"

He sighed, the exhale tickling my neck. "It's a hard question to answer, honey."

I huffed. "How many times—"

He pinched my nipple, cutting me off in mid-sentence. "I'm pretty sure that you just admitted a little bit ago that you *are* mine. So, that makes you my honey. Get used to it."

Slapping his roaming hand with my free one, I wiggled fruitlessly to get extricate myself from his hold. "And as *I* remember it, I said this'll only happen 'til you're gone!"

With a little maneuvering and quick reflexes on his part, I was on my tummy with my hands pinned to my side within seconds. His body covered mine as he kissed me all over my shoulders and neck. Moving up to nip and lick at my ear, it wasn't long before I squirmed beneath him, my hands itching to touch him and make him hot like he made me so easily.

The devilish chuckle in my ear as he guided himself to me below made me still. He leaned in, his words harsh, raw.

"Here's the thing, Ellie. You *are* mine," he reiterated, hissing as he entered me just a little and stopped. "I don't know what happened all those years ago. And maybe I shouldn't have walked away but I wasn't willing to stand there, watching you waste away before me any longer." Another inch forward. "Five long years I've regretted it. I let my mother give you that house because I foolishly hoped - wished really - that even if it was another few decades, the gift of that house would bring you back to me."

At that, he thrust deep and stopped. I was speechless at his words, the only sound a moan as he wrapped his arms around me. He didn't stop there, though.

"We both made mistakes. I can't say I knew what was going on with you because I didn't. The way I see it, the both of us have been give another chance to try again, to make things better. We can never go back to what we were, never fix things. We can move forward though. Won't you give me a second chance?"

I really didn't want to cry again, yet my throat closed with panic as tears sprung to my eyes. He was putting himself out there and all I wanted to do was shake my head. Deny it, deny him. Deny us.

Going backwards wasn't what I wanted, was it?

For once, I didn't know but as I spoke, I heard the bitterness I'd kept locked up the past five years seep into my voice. "It doesn't work like that, Stefan. I've changed...you've changed. I'm not sure trying again is worth it."

He withdrew slowly, tortuously. "Ah, but that's where you're wrong honey. If I think you're worth waiting potential decades for, then I'd say I'm a pretty good risk. And your body is certainly not complaining."

It wasn't, but my body was a traitor. I shook my head. "I'm not convinced..."

"Good thing I've got time to persuade you then."

After that, his seduction left me speechless. Which was probably a good thing because I may have been tempted to tell him exactly what he wanted to hear. And I wasn't ready for that.

I wasn't sure I ever would be.

# CHAPTER TEN

The day of Stefan's return home came quickly.

Without work, I spent much of the previous week packing up most of my personal items while researching moving companies and their prices. Because my move was across the country, the most expedient form of moving meant shipping everything and then just driving there. It would take me about three days, but a little alone time to myself seemed like a great plan.

Stefan, on the other hand, had helped me pack a little but otherwise spent the week working - either on his computer, or on his phone. Several times he had gone outside to take a call and it left me rather curious as to the caller's identity. He'd always come back with a smile though and apologize for being so rude.

It was hard not to like him. And I really put some effort into it.

Sitting at the dining room table, I didn't even blink when the door opened, Stefan returning from his run. He headed straight to the shower after nodding at me and I went back to reading my book. He'd asked me earlier in the week if I would take him to the airport and I really didn't have a reason to say no.

His flight was in three hours so we had to leave pretty soon. He didn't take long though and when he walked out of the bathroom wearing nothing, I stared. He winked at me.

"How about one final quickie?"

My body hummed to life at his words. Tamping down the impulse to say yes, I sent him what I hoped came across as a 'dirty' and 'you wish' look. "We don't have time. Your flight leaves at ten."

"I suppose you're right," he said with a sigh. "Give me a few moments."

He walked back into the room a few moments later, buttoning up his shirt. At the touch on my shoulder, I looked up to find him smiling. Nodding at my e-reader, he asked, "What are you reading?"

"A book."

"Oh, you're funny. What's it about?"

"Nothing you'd be interested in. It's a romance novel."

He rolled his eyes. "If I wasn't interested, I wouldn't ask. Now, title?"

Huffing, I turned it off and set it on the table. "If you must know, it's called 'The Healing Heart' and you wouldn't know the author."

"Again, what's it about?"

I didn't dare stand up, although his close proximity as his hand rested on my shoulder made me wish I'd taken him up on his offer for one final time to be close to him. "It's a romance, what do ya think? Either way, it's upbeat and happy and just feel good. No drama, no angst, just love."

"Ugh." He smiled down at me even with the sound of disgust. "So what you're saying is, it's not realistic. Let me guess. The hero is completely amazing and has no faults? And I bet the heroine is the same too, huh?"

I scowled and stood up, my hands on his chest as I pushed him away from me gently. "You're an ass."

"Come on!" He laughed as I put the device in my purse. "There's no such thing as a man with no faults."

"You're the expert."

"Ouch! I'm wounded!" A hand up to his heart, I smiled at his antics. "Ah, see. You *can't* resist my charms."

I sighed. "Ready to go now?"

"What's the paragons name?"

"It's just a book!" I didn't understand why he cared, but he just stared at me until I answered. "Conley."

"Wow, unique."

I couldn't tell if that was sarcasm. "You don't think someone can just be a good person and not have any major faults. Or nothing wrong with them?"

"No way." He crossed his arms over his chest. "Everybody is screwed up in one way or another."

"That's quite negative of you. I'd like to believe there are people like that who exist."

"Tell you what," he uttered, leaning forward to brush a light kiss across my lips. "You find that perfect man and I'll eat my words."

I said nothing, just lifted a brow as he stepped away and packed up his laptop.

Fifteen minutes later, we were on our way out the door. Putting the stuff into the trunk, he held his hand out.

"Let me drive," he begged, giving me a cute puppy dog look that I couldn't resist. "I promise I'll drive slow."

Rolling my eyes, I handed him the keys. Besides, I wasn't quite awake yet so I really didn't mind if he drove. "Please, don't drive slow. You are already going to be there less than two hours before your flight."

"You're the boss, honey!"

I let him get away with the endearment as I climbed into the passengers seat.

Backing out of the parking space, he grabbed my hand in his once we were on the road. "So, do you know what you will do when you've moved back?"

"Nope!"

The highway was only a few minutes from my house and as he took the on-ramp, I jerked my hand from his. "You're going the wrong way! Turn around!"

"Am I?" He squinted at the sign and then laughed. "You're right, I am. Whoops."

Focusing my eyes on his face, a sudden feeling of dread filled my chest. My gut instinct had to be mistaken. "Whoops? Turn around right now!"

I swear, his eyes twinkled right in that moment. I wasn't one to believe such tripe usually, but his whole face lit up with amusement. "Absolutely not."

"You're going to miss your flight!"

He busted out laughing and I knew the joke was on me. "I never had a return flight, Ellie. I admit, you losing your job sucked but it was like divine intervention! When you said you'd drive me to the airport, I knew just what to do."

"Do? Do what? Kidnap me?"

He threw me a look of admonishment. "Don't be silly. You're not a kid and you're certainly not napping." Then he winked.

Gaping at him, I couldn't believe this was happening. I really couldn't. The Stefan I used to know would have never dared this. Who the hell was this provoking man? I took a deep breath. It's not like I could jump out on the highway so escaping wasn't an option.

"Where are we going? I don't even have any clothes!"

He didn't look away from the road. "We're going home. And of course you have clothes, they are in the trunk."

"You little...," I stopped myself, huffing. "When the hell did you pack me clothing?"

"When you were sleeping. I admit, I'm shocked you didn't notice some of your clothes were missing."

I felt my face heat. I honestly had so much clothing I didn't even know what all the items were in my wardrobe. It was my only vice - and it was an expensive one. "What about my stuff? My apartment?"

He chuckled then. "All taken care of. The moving company will come tomorrow and pack up all the rest of your stuff. It will be delivered next week."

"What? Did you pay them? Can you even afford that?" My voice rose with incredulity. "Why would you do this?"

He sighed. "Of course I paid them, quite handsomely I might add - which obviously means I can afford it."

"And you did this because...you thought me so enthralled with you that you didn't even stop to think I wanted to do it myself?"

"Nope. I'm not that delusional."

I almost cracked a smile at that. Scowling to prevent it from slipping through, I tapped my hands on my legs. "Well? Why then?"

"Because I thought a road trip would be fun."

"That's it?"

"Yep!"

"You are so infuriating!"

"Thanks, so are you. Now sit back and relax because we won't be stopping for a while."

Crossing my arms over my chest in a fit of pique, I stared out the window and wondered what the hell I was gonna do now.

~*~

I opened my eyes as the car slowed. Rubbing the initial blurriness away, I noticed it was getting dark outside. We'd only stopped for gas and food once. Looking around, the brightness of the lights had me blinking rapidly as I looked down again. Great, now I was seeing stars.

"Where are we?" I asked with a scowl as I sat up straight. "Hopefully a place to rest. My ass hurts."

"Yes, Ellie. You are so impatient," Stefan replied with a chuckle. "I figured we could stop here and then in the morning, we will go gambling!"

"Gambling? Why?"

His eyes widened, staring at me as if I'd grown two heads. "Why not?"

"Plenty of reasons." As I checked out the building, my mouth fell open. "This place is huge!"

"A hotel and casino all in one." He shut the car off and climbed out before I could reply.

We were out of the car and into the hotel within minutes.

The lobby area was pretty empty. When Stefan walked up to the counter, I stood there, taking in the interior. The double doors straight ahead were closed and I could hear people cheering and laughing. Gathering that the doors led straight to the casino, I joined Stefan as the man handed him a key.

"Only one key? Where is mine for my room?"

Stefan grabbed my arm gently as the bell hop put the luggage we'd carried in on a cart and headed toward the elevator. We followed.

"We are staying in the same room," he whispered, having leaned in close to my ear. "After all, weren't you the one worried about my finances? Maybe I can't afford another room."

"Yeah, but I can!" I snapped at him, trying to tug my arm from his grasp and failing. "Let me go pay for my own!"

As the elevator door opened, the bellhop entered and then held it open.

"There aren't any more rooms. At least, not this late in the evening. Get in."

Annoyed with his bossiness, I succeed in pulling my arm from his grasp as we got into the elevator. As I watched the numbers climb, I felt ill. "How far is it?"

He must have heard something in my voice. Pulling me into his embrace, he ran his hand over my hair as I closed my eyes to try and calm the panic climbing in my throat. It wasn't that I minded elevators; in small doses, they were fine but this felt as if it were taking forever.

"Top floor. Damn it, I'm sorry. I forgot you have a fear of small places."

Top floor? Well that would explain my panic. But...wasn't that usually the biggest and most expensive room in a hotel?

I started to wonder then who this man was, focusing on my thoughts rather than the small enclosure. A room on the top level of a hotel - and one with a casino at that - was not cheap, even for only one evening. Not afford another room my ass. Looked as if he'd be answering some questions from me later.

Trying to ignore the fact we were on an elevator didn't last long and I glanced up at the numbers as they pinged. When it finally stopped, I pushed Stefan away and darted off as fast as I could manage. Standing against the wall, I did my controlled breathing techniques to try and calm down as he opened the door to the room. The bellhop put the luggage inside and left after Stefan tipped him.

Stefan gestured for me to go inside ahead of him. I couldn't resist a jibe as I walked past.

"You must have planned my abduction quite in advance. No way you got this room when we were just standing in—" My words were cut off by the gorgeous room in front of my eyes.

He chuckled behind me as he closed the door. "Nice, isn't it?"

Yeah, it was. But I'd never admit that to him. Turning around, I waved my hand around lazily while flashing him what I hoped was a disinterested look. "It'll do, I suppose."

"See? Why don't you take that attitude about me?"

Tilting my head to the side, I studied him. For a man who had been in the car all day, he looked fairly put together and not at all rumpled. The opposite of me. I felt disheveled and icky, which wasn't helped by the fact I'd not showered that morning. I knew who I could blame for that.

Crossing my arms, I raised a brow at him. "I sure hope you aren't serious."

"Of course not." He picked up two of the bags and headed toward the back of the suite. Assuming it was the bedroom, I didn't follow.

The suite was huge. There was a kitchen and a living room right in view of where I stood. The furthest wall boasted of glass only, leading out to a lovely view that blew the one from my apartment window away.

"When did you reserve this room, Stefan?" I yelled to him in the other room. When he didn't answer, I turned to go to him and saw him walking toward me. "Well?"

"You're nosy," he said with a scowl, only to ruin it with a smile two seconds later. "On the day after you lost your job. Before you say 'oh my god, you planned this' I will say...obviously. I had to."

No wonder he'd walked outside so many times during his visit. Sneaky bastard.

Pretending I didn't care, I flipped my hair over my shoulder and shrugged. "I have to get a shower. Where is the bag you packed for me?"

He pointed to the one by the door. "Right there, honey. It's all yours. Enjoy your shower, I'm gonna make me something to drink!"

"Gee thanks." I walked over to the door and picked up the bag as he went into the kitchen.

I couldn't wait to see what kind of clothing he'd packed for me.

# CHAPTER ELEVEN

Wrapped in a towel, I searched through my bags for something *not* sexy to wear.

I wasn't surprised by his selection. Lacy underwear, a silk nightgown, skirts, blouses, pantyhose and a few pair of high heels of assorted colors that also happened to coordinate well with all the outfits he'd put together in the bag. I'd give it to him; he certainly didn't lack for a sense of style.

Then, I had a wonderful idea. Seeing his luggage that he brought into the room before I went to take a shower, I stalked over to his bags and opened them, a wicked grin on my face.

After getting dressed, I brushed out my hair and left it hanging to dry faster. It naturally curled a little when left to it's own devices, which I usually helped along by putting it up in a bun.

Stepping out into the living room, I stopped and cleared my throat. "How do I look?"

Stefan's wicked grin dropping to a frown as he saw my outfit was priceless. "What the hell? Why are you wearing my clothes?"

I wore a pair of his lounge pants and a baggy t-shirt. He wasn't built but he was certainly bigger than me. I definitely wasn't wearing anything I'd consider sexy and busted out laughing as his scowl deepened. "This is what you get for not packing me bottoms!"

Then the mischievous smile was back and he walked up to me with intent. Oh yes, it was clear in his eyes what he wanted.

"You think that wearing my clothes will make you less attractive? You could wear a trash bag and I'd still want to f—"

He was cut off by the knock at the door.

*Saved in just the knick of time!* Despite my curiosity about who was here, I took the opportunity to get away and went over to the couch, plopping down on it with moan of pleasure at the softness against my bottom. Sitting for hours in a car had never suited me; the lack of movement and ability to get comfortable never sufficed.

Turning on the television, I smelled the tasty scent of pizza at the exact moment Stefan took the seat next to me. Placing the pizza on the table, he rubbed his hands together with what could only be described as glee. As I bit into my slice, he bit into his and let out a moan.

I swallowed my piece, then laughed. "Why are you acting as if you haven't had pizza in ages?" My memory clearly recalled a man who declared he 'would die if he had to give up pizza' so his delight at eating it amused me to no end.

"I haven't," he admitted, before taking another bite and winking at me.

"How is that possible? You were always so adamant that you'd never, *ever* give up pizza."

99

He shrugged as he polished off that piece and reached for another. "People change."

Indeed. I wanted to say something snarky but for once, I decided against it. We were stuck together for at least two more days and since this had become a free vacation for me, I didn't want to ruin the peace we'd fallen into.

Scrolling through the channels as I finished off my slice of pizza, I grinned as I stumbled upon the perfect torture in place of the cutting retort just begging to be let out. "Oh look, *honey*," I emphasized with a super sweet voice. "*Dirty Dancing* is on!"

He jerked his eyes toward the television, groaning as his eyes came into contact with Jennifer Grey and Patrick Swayze on the screen, practicing the dance moves. Baby giggling every time Johnny would side swipe her boob always made me smile.

"Please, turn it off!"

As he tried to snatch the remote, I jumped up and took off, squealing. Standing on one side of the table, I turned it up louder until the music was clearly heard across the room. Stefan stood at the opposite end, ready to catch me if I tried to escape.

"Ellie, turn it down!"

"No fucking way!" I swayed back and forth, holding the remote above my head even as I stared straight at him, grinning. "I see you have no qualms about sticking me in a corner though. Tsk tsk!"

I caught him trying not to smile even as he darted around the side of the table. I took off back toward the couch, laughing.

"You're not the only one who got in shape, buddy!"

Singing at the top of my lungs, I danced with the remote even as the music ended and they talked on the movie. He still stood a bit away from me, his arms crossed over his chest. The sudden grin on his face made my heart speed up, his hands going to the buttons on his shirt and undoing them, one by one. I paused in my dancing and just watched, transfixed.

Dropping the shirt on the floor, he pounced at me. With a squeak, I dropped the remote and ran toward the bedroom. At the sudden silence in the other room, I slipped behind the door and waited for him to come through.

Entering the room, he must have realized my game as he didn't turn the light on.

"Oh gee, I wonder where Ellie could possibly be," he said in an exaggerated whisper. "Come out, come out, wherever you are!"

*Nice try.* I wasn't gonna laugh and give away my spot.

The slightest bit of light gave me an advantage and I couldn't help but ogle him as he headed toward the closet. Stefan seriously had to be the sexiest man I'd ever seen. Even if he wasn't overly muscled, you could still see the strength in his arms and back from the small amount of working out he did. The sight of him shirtless made my body burn with anticipation.

Seeing my chance to surprise him, I moved out from behind the door as he opened the closet ones and ambushed him.

"Got ya!" I whooped as I put my arms around his shoulders and he stiffened. "Now you are my prisoner!"

"Yeah?" His voice came out deep, silky. "And what are you going to do with me?"

I heard the smile in his voice, both of us knowing it wouldn't take much for the tables to turn. He could overpower me with ease. Yet he didn't move a muscle, standing there in my arms. I'm sure he tried to anticipate my next move, so I decided to shock him.

Circling him in a slow, deliberate manner, I traced his shoulder with one finger, going down his arm as I stopped in front of him. Running the hand down his chest, I heard him suck in a breath as it stopped on the button to his jeans. Unsnapping the fly, I slid my hand in just enough to tease and laughed.

"Already excited, I see."

"Told you the clothing wouldn't put me off. You're sexy in anything," he ground out. I could only imagine how much self-control it took for him to just stand there, with my hand kept just out of reach to where he wanted my touch most.

I enjoyed every second we stood there, both still as stone, breathing heavily.

Then, I moved, placing a hand on each side of his face and went up on tiptoe. Our lips inches away from each other, I whispered.

"Bedtime."

~*~

Within seconds, Stefan's arms were around my waist, his mouth on mine.

I knew he wouldn't let me escape. He'd caught me in his web, his strong, warm arms like a cocoon I never wanted to leave. As he tried to gain entrance to my mouth, his hands slid under the shirt to cup my breasts in his hand. I sighed and let him in.

This is why I didn't like to let him touch me. Once he did, my heart screamed to stay while my brain yelled for me to get away. And my body, my body was the biggest betrayer of all. It was in cahoots with my heart and I wasn't happy about that.

Not because he was untrustworthy or because he had walked away.

I'd done that to him. I was the one who couldn't be trusted to act like an adult.

In my fear, I'd pushed away someone who loved me and had stopped loving myself.

The thoughts send a wave of nausea as my head began to spin. I knew what was happening. I was having a panic attack and I didn't want him to witness it.

Yanking my lips away from his, I pushed on his shoulders. "Let me go! Right fucking now, let go!"

He backed away, his hands up even as I could see the concern on his face. "What's wrong?"

Taking deep breaths, I bent over, feeling as if I'd just taken part in a marathon. Hoping the feeling would go away. But it kept hitting me and as my hand continued to spin as my stomach roiled, I turned and ran to the bathroom.

"Ellie! What the hell!"

I heard him yell even as I closed the bathroom door, locking it. Sliding down to the floor, I tried to calm down.

Why now? I hadn't had one in several years. It was worse than I remember. But maybe it was because my past was on the opposite side of the door, voice full of worry. It seemed like all I did was cause him to worry.

I didn't want to tell him the truth. I didn't want him to look at me and think how disgusting I was for what I'd done. Maybe he wouldn't have cared. Maybe he would have been believed me when I said I'd been raped. I couldn't remember for sure though and that irritated me. I knew I had been while knocked out and I also knew I'd been blessed to have no memory of it. That didn't calm me, however, and never had.

Feeling the tears stream down my face, I rocked back and forth as I sobbed.

He pounded and pounded on the door, but I just cried.

Cried for the girl who thought she'd done the right thing.

For woman who had chosen to deal with it on her own.

And for the man on the opposite side of the door who had no clue what I'd gone through. Who I'd pushed away because I hadn't known how to deal with my own feelings about the situation.

Who still loved me, even after the way I'd treated him.

And as the knocking continued, I cried harder.

"Please Ellie, let me in," he begged. "I don't know why you're crying and you don't have to tell me. Just come out and let me hold you."

Was that all it would take?

"Come out honey. I'll even watch *Dirty Dancing* with you if you want."

I laughed through my tears, which only fell harder.

I hated that I needed him right that moment, that he could make me laugh through my tears and even after he'd walked away from me, he was the one I dreamed about. The only man I'd ever loved.

"I'm not going anywhere, so you might as well just come out."

I knew his words were true. He'd come this far, he certainly wouldn't give up now. I gave in.

Standing up, I went over and blew my nose, running cool water over my face as I examined my swollen eyes in the mirror. Walking over to the door, I swung it open and there he stood, waiting for me.

No smile, no frown.

He opened his arms to comfort me if I desired it, watching me intently with eyes full of concern.

So I stepped into them and as his arms enveloped me, I said the one thing I should have said when I first saw him again in that airport.

"I'm sorry, Stefan. I'm so, so sorry."

As the tears fell from my eyes once more, I felt him relax, knowing he knew what I meant.

Stroking my hair with one hand, he kissed my cheek. "I know honey. No need to be sorry. I always knew you'd come back to me one day."

In that moment, I was glad he'd had faith all these years because I'd so obviously lost mine in that alley six years ago.

# CHAPTER TWELVE

We didn't end up gambling the next morning. I wasn't really up for it and Stefan made it clear that we could do it another time.

After staying up cuddling a while and watching some television, we'd gone to bed. Snuggled up against each other, I tried to find the resolve to admit to him what had happened all those years ago. Deciding I would tell him once we were back in town, I slept better than I had in a long time.

I made my goal for the rest of the drive into a simple one - enjoy our time together. We left the hotel by eleven a.m. and headed out. The sun was shining brightly and we were both in a cheerful mood.

"So, what are your plans when you get back?" He winked at me. "I hope I'm one of them."

"I don't really have plans other than getting settled in. Oh, except to go see Grace and her daughter Lyndsey."

He looked over at me, brows furrowed with confusion. "You still talk to Grace?"

"Heck yeah. I mean, we went for a little while without talking but she's always been there for me."

Concentrating on the road, he just nodded at my answer.

"She lives in town. Don't you ever see her?"

"Yeah, I guess you could say I do. It's not like her and I were ever close so it's not like we're buddy-buddy."

True. Even though she'd been my roomie, we hadn't really hung out in a group setting.

"Her daughter is so pretty! I've seen tons of pics of her over the years. I can't believe how time flies."

I felt his hand on mine seconds before he turned it over, interlocking our fingers and squeezing. "She is a cutie," he agreed.

The silence, for the first time since I'd seen him, didn't bother me. It was a companionable one. The kind of moment you hope for in your later years of life with a partner who just got you.

That was us. We just got each other.

Even though he didn't know the secret, he still understood me. In my grief, I had forgotten that.

The scenery flew by and the peace that had been building inside my chest was still growing. I was excited to go home. I wasn't so thrilled to face my past, but it was time I stopped running from it.

Hopefully, I'd tell Stefan and he would understand. Then we could move on with our lives.

We both jumped when my phone rang. Seeing it was my mother, I didn't answer at first. When it rang again just moments later, I sighed.

"Hi, mom."

"Elizabeth! Where have you been?"

She sounded panicked and I answered before thinking. "Uhm, well, I'm kinda in a car on my way there. Why?"

"I've been calling but it just went straight to voice-mail. What do you mean you're on your way here?"

"It means I'm coming home."

I had told her I'd lost my job and might end up moving back home. Guess I'd forgotten to mention to her that was absolutely going to do so. Not shocking since telling her my every move had ended once I'd left home at eighteen.

"Oh, I see. When will you be here? And why are you driving?"

"Because I need my car? There are movers that will pack up my house."

"Okay. Well, I'll see you then, right?"

"Yes mom, you will. I'll talk to you later."

"Bye."

She hung up and I had never felt so awkward in my life. That was how our conversations always were. She wanted to know where I was and how I was doing, yet never seemed to have anything else to say. That was my fault though and I knew it. The talk with her about what happened long ago was going to be a difficult one.

"She cares about you, y'know."

Looking over at Stefan, I grimaced. "I know, but she's got a funny way of showing it."

He shrugged. "I think we've all got our own funny ways of showing we care."

Laughing, I pulled my hand from his. "Yeah, I suppose that's true." I leaned back against my seat and closed my eyes.

"Taking a nap already?"

"Nah, just relaxing my eyes," I assured him. "So, tell me, what have you been doing all these years?"

"What do you mean? With work?"

"Sure. With work."

I heard the amusement in his voice as he responded. "I worked at the company I was at when you left for about a year. Then, I decided to start my own company, which is quite the competitor in software engineering. I have three offices across the country now."

Impressive. He'd been busy. "What's it called?"

"Well, I went lofty just for giggles. So it's called 'Pierce & Pierce Enterprise' which my mother found hilarious."

"Hah, I'm sure she did! Why Pierce & Pierce when there is only one of you?"

"Nah, my brother Evan works there as well."

"I see. So that's how you could afford that room in the hotel, I take it."

He threw me a grin, not saying anything before looking back at the road.

"And you've been single the whole time?"

"Ha! No way. I did some dating here and there, but nothing serious. I went a little crazy for a little while though," he paused, his hesitation about continuing that line of thought more than evident.

"Go on. It's not like we were dating."

"Well, I tried to forget you. I also drank a lot. Neither was a good way to do that, I assure you."

"So you were being a drunk man-slut is what you're saying."

"Uh...well, no. I didn't sleep around like that, I just got really drunk and made an ass of myself." He cleared his throat. "Did you date anybody else?"

I chuckled. "Yeah, one person last year. That was it. I spent a lot of years in therapy before attempting to date again."

"Really? You should ask for your money back."

"Funny." I reached an arm out and blindly slapped at his arm. "It actually helped me a lot!"

He laughed and grabbed it, kissing the top of my hand before releasing it. "I'm sure it did. What was his name?"

"Geoffrey. He was okay. We slept together but it wasn't very good." Then I mentally slapped myself. Why had I offered up that information?

"That's too bad," he remarked, even as I knew he had to be smiling at the fact he was the only other man I'd ever slept with. "How did you two meet?"

"Not that its any of your business, but we met in my therapist's office."

"Romantic."

With a laugh, I shrugged even though he couldn't see me. "It didn't last long anyway."

He didn't say anything and I was glad for the end of that conversation. My relationship with Geoffrey wasn't really something I wanted to discuss with anybody really. Yet, I knew now that Stefan owned his own business and was obviously doing really well.

The silence stretched and with that, the combination of beautiful scenery and the peaceful quiet in the car had me drifting off as the radio played softly, Stefan humming along.

~*~

One more hotel stay - sans sex - and another long drive later, we arrived in our hometown.

As we passed the downtown area, my leg shook, giving away how nervous I was. It had been one

110

thing to declare my intent to face my past; it was another to actually arrive here and see it for myself.

"You okay?"

I had driven away from the hotel that morning, wanting to give him a break from driving. I wasn't really great with directions, but Stefan had been patient and we'd only got turned around once when I wasn't paying attention. However, after lunch, he had gotten behind the wheel again and I'd taken a nap.

"Yeah, I'm fine," I replied, unable to see much outside the window because it was so dark. "Where are we going?"

"Well, I'm taking you to your new home. However, I'm hoping you'll let me stay the night and drive me to my place in the morning. Otherwise I'm going to have to walk there."

I smiled to myself, part of me liking the idea even though I'd never do that.

"Where is your car?"

"In my driveway. Evan drove me to the airport."

"Oh I see. Then he knew you were coming to see me?"

"I think everybody in town knew that I was coming to visit you."

"Visit me? You meant to drag me back here by the hair if you could manage it," I retorted, even as I smiled.

"Last I checked, you enjoyed having that lovely brown hair pulled on," he said with a laugh. "Besides, what else is a man to do with the woman he's meant to be with when she won't do as she's bid?"

"Do as I'm bid? Please!" I rolled my eyes, even though he couldn't see the motion. "Next you'll say I should be in the kitchen naked, barefoot and pregnant!"

"Nah. You'll have an apron at least. Can't have my woman shivering while cooking me some bacon."

At that, my eyes teared up as uncontrollable laughter took over. Pressing a fist to my lips, I tried to stifle it, although Stefan had joined in. When he pulled into the driveway of the house, I sucked in a deep breath to try and calm down.

Rubbing my face with my hands, I had sufficiently soothed my mirth as he turned on the lights inside the car. Turning toward me, he smiled and I struggled to keep a straight face, lest I burst out laughing once again.

"So, am I allowed to stay the night?"

I knew that would get me, him staying the night. Even though I had told him we could only sleep together before our return, I knew it wouldn't stop there. But if it was going to be this way, then it would be my way.

"Depends."

He reached over and took my hands in his. My stomach fluttered with anticipation, breathless as he kissed them and lingered, a smile peeking through the serious look on his face.

"And what does it depend on, honey?"

"This is all I can give you right now," I stated, my own words sobering in contrast to the joking about being his woman. "I-I can't promise anything else, not even a relationship with you. I'm not sure that will ever happen."

He nodded. "I understand. It doesn't mean I can't try to convince you otherwise though, does it?"

"No," I whispered, the idea of him trying to persuade me sent a thrill of excitement through me. "No, it doesn't."

At my words, he leaned in, bringing one hand up behind my neck to tug my face closer.

Brushing his lips across mine softly, he smiled against my mouth.

"Good, because I'm not sure I could resist trying to sway you in my direction," he confessed, removing his hand and tucking stray hair behind my ear. "Now, let's get you inside so we can get some rest."

And with that, we were out of the car and into the house within minutes.

I wondered if I'd just signed my body over to the one man who would use it to get exactly what he wanted.

Me. My heart. My devotion, once again.

The idea didn't feel me with as much dread as it had just days before.

A fact that now terrified me all on its own.

~*~

Stefan's body was still wrapped around mine when I awoke the next morning.

Both of us exhausted from the drive, it hadn't taken long for either of us to undress and pass out after we'd crawled into the bed. He cuddled my body against his, threw his leg over mine and wrapped his arms around my waist.

The last thing I remembered from the previous evening had been his lips gently kissing my neck just before he whispered 'goodnight, love' to me.

His breathing still deep and even, I knew I'd have to wake him soon. I didn't even know what time it was, but my mother expected me to arrive some time today. Taking advantage of the opportunity to explore his form, I slid my hand down his arm, which was bare and silky with a light dusting of dark red hair that matched the hair on his head.

He murmured behind me, pulling me tighter against his body as he snuggled into my back. Chuckling, I wiggled my bottom in response.

"If you don't stop that, you'll find yourself adding a moan to that wiggle," he growled, the remnants of slumber apparent in his words.

"Well, let me up. I need to—" He moved his body before I could finish my sentence and I dashed off the bed.

Returning a few minutes later, he was still lying in the bed on his back, the blanket barely covering his naked bottom half. Walking over to the bed, I bent until our faces nearly touched.

"Time to get up, princess," I said with a laugh.

He'd always hated when I called him that. When he didn't respond, I poked him in the abdomen.

In a flash, he grabbed me by the waist and yanked my body on top of his so I was lying the length of him.

"Hey!" I struggled to get free, only to have his hands tighten as he stiffened. "Let me go!"

He opened his eyes slowly, a cocky grin on his face. "You called me 'princess' - that can't go unpunished."

*Uh oh.*

"No! No! I'm sorry!" I continued fighting, even though I knew it to be fruitless.

I knew what was coming. He had never liked when I called him that, yet I'd still do it on purpose. Just as I had moments ago. I'd asked for him and damned if I wasn't going to relish it. I buried my face in his chest, biting back a smile so he wouldn't know how much I planned to enjoy this.

His left arm pinned my upper body to his. He lifted his right hand and brought it down on my ass.

I howled even as my heart sped up, the sting of his hand sending tendrils of pleasure through that region. Still squirming to get free, he wrapped his right leg around the bottom of my legs to keep me stationary before bringing his hand down again and again.

Then, he was rubbing the area soothingly with his hand, grinding against me.

"I've wanted to do that since I first saw you in the airport," he stated, his own voice thick with desire. "You've no idea."

I did though. My body practically hummed with excitement, his words making my stomach tighten with an answering lust    . I'd practically been begging for it since the moment I'd opened my mouth; begging for him to do what he'd always done, what he'd invariably been able to do to me.

Rocking against him, I pushed against his chest and he moved his arm, letting me sit up.

Reaching down, I grabbed him in my hand. His eyes closed on a moan even as his hands grabbed my hips, squeezing. Lifting up slightly, I put him in place, slowly sliding down. I heard him gritting his teeth, the grip on my hips almost painful in his attempts to let me have control. I moaned at the exquisite bliss, the sensations making me tingle all over as our bodies met fully.

Stefan brought a hand down to me and played as I lifted up again. Hanging at the edge, I teased him by rotating my hips. Groaning, he surged up even as he pulled my hips down, burying himself to the hilt. My turn to gasp and moan then. Before I can lift again, he sits up and rolls me over onto my back.

"Wrap your legs around me, honey," he instructed with an urgency I shared.

Doing as he said, he brought his mouth down to mine, forcing my lips open with a thrust of his tongue. Kissing him back, I savored every bit of the moment, alternating between caresses to his back and the dig of my nails into it. His lovemaking had slowed, making love to my mouth along with the rest of my body as he moved in and out at a leisurely pace.

My breasts were crushed against his chest, the light dusting of hair on his teasing my nipples and making them harden, the sensation bordering on painful. Impatient at his slow pacing, I ripped my lips away and kissed his shoulder before biting it.

He hissed out a breath before laughing. "Problem, honey?"

When I bucked against him, he grabbed my ass with one hand and withdrew before sliding home again, even slower this time.

"Please…" I begged. I couldn't wait anymore and I didn't care if I had to plead.

"Please what? What do you want, Ellie?"

"Go faster!"

He grinned even as he stopped moving, the warmth of it echoed in the husky timbre.

"Only if you promise to tell me your secret soon." Capturing my wide eyes with his triumphant ones, he brought a hand up to cup my cheek. "I know it's something big, Ellie, and I deserve to know."

He didn't say anything else, beginning to move again even as he kept his eyes locked on mine.

Licking my sudden dry lips, I felt tears spring to my eyes. "I'm scared. It's been so long..."

"It's okay honey. Whatever it is, I can handle it."

"You promise?" I wanted to believe him, to trust that he'd understand, but I'd told myself the opposite for so long.

"As long as you promise to tell me, Ellie. I will handle it...*we* will handle it. Okay?"

I nodded and he took my mouth with his again, giving me exactly what I wanted with a speed that left me breathless.

# CHAPTER THIRTEEN

Dropping Stefan off at home with the promise to 'have the talk' later that evening, I drove to the grocery store.

The wonderful thing about small towns is that not much ever really changes. The early hour - seven a.m. - meant that the lack of shoppers made for a nice quiet moment to myself. Soon, I headed home.

Driving past Grace's place - the same place we had shared all those years ago - I slowed down as the front door opened and a man stepped into it. Not wanting to be too obvious I kept driving even though Grace had never seen this car. I gasped as I recognized who she kissed just as I drove out of their sight.

None other than Stefan's brother, Evan.

Turning the corner, I parked and picked up my phone, dialing.

"Hello?" Grace answered, her voice breathy.

"Well hi there," I replied, grinning. "Are you having a nice morning?"

"Oh, hey Elizabeth. I've just been relaxing since Lyndsey is with my mother this weekend. How are you?"

"Got back into town last night, went shopping this morning. On my way home, mind if I stop by?"

She was silent for a moment. "Sure, how long?"

"Just a couple minutes. See ya then."

Grace hung up without replying.

Sitting in my car for a few minutes, I wondered if she was going to tell me about Evan. Did Stefan know? I'd have to ask her.

I drove off and went around the block so I came in from the right direction, just in case she was watching.

Why would I even think such a thing? She had no reason to believe I saw anything. Rolling my eyes at myself, I pulled into her now empty driveway.

She opened the door as I walked up the steps. She'd changed her clothing style - it was definitely more of what I considered mom style with jeans and a t-shirt than the Grace I knew years ago who dressed up on a daily basis, no matter what activity she had planned for the day. The difference shocked me, even though I knew it shouldn't. People changed, Stefan had said, and obviously it was more true than I wanted to admit.

Smiling at me, she stepped back. "Come on in! It's so good to see you when it's not over Skype!"

I walked past her and she shut the door. We hadn't seen each other in person since I'd left, but her enthusiasm at seeing me seemed a bit forced. At least, I thought so. It had been so long, perhaps I simply remained out of touch with in person body language. Yeah, that had to be it.

"I can't stay for long since I went shopping," I replied, making sure my voice didn't betray the troubles in my mind. "I just wanted to stop in for a few minutes."

Okay, my intent was nosiness, but I wasn't going to say that out loud to her.

"Well, do you want a quick cup of tea?"

I nodded, relieved that she seemed oblivious to the tension. "That would be great, thanks."

We headed to the kitchen and I took a seat while she flitted around preparing the tea.

"So how is Lyndsey?"

She threw me a real smile over her shoulder as she put the electric kettle on. "She's her usual bubbly self. She's getting to the age where she has a reply for everything I say. No matter what I say, for that matter."

"Basically, she's a little mini you?" I asked, laughing.

"Ha, ha, yeah! She's definitely got my attitude."

The silence following it seemed awkward. I didn't like it. This was the first time since before I left where our friendship seemed that way. Grace still faced away from me and I wondered if anybody knew about her dating Evan. Unable to resist asking, I kept my voice light and cheery as I spoke.

"You seeing anyone? It's been a long time for you, hasn't it?"

And for the first time in our friendship, Grace lied to me.

She shrugged. "Nope, I can't say I am. Been so busy with Lyndsey and focusing on work."

I didn't give away that I knew she lied because I wanted to figure out why she'd do such a thing. "Aw, that's too bad."

"Not really. I've survived this long without a man, surely I don't need one now right?" She opened up the cupboard and reached in.

"I suppose. I thought the same thing, but I think Stefan and I might work things out," I answered with a smile, my mouth going dry at the confession. I hadn't planned to say anything but she was my friend and I wanted to share even though I knew her feelings about him.

I jumped when the mug she was holding hit the counter with a distinct reaction of surprise. Grace whirled around, glaring at me.

"You've got to be kidding me!"

Irritated at the reaction, even though I'd expected it, I grinned. "Nope, I'm not! You should just be happy for me."

She huffed. Huffed! "I'm sorry, but I can't be. You two aren't good for each other."

I titled my head to the side and lifted a brow at her. "That isn't what you said when he and I were engaged."

"What I said was wrong," she snapped back, whirling around to face the counter again. "It was a long time ago, too."

Her vehemence did shock me then. This went way beyond her just not liking him for leaving me and my chest burned with sudden anger. I could see her hands shaking as she poured the hot water into the mugs. Not wanting her to burn herself, I waited until she finished pouring before I spoke, no longer willing to bite my tongue.

"I saw you, Grace. I saw you kissing Evan because I drove by as he was coming out the door. If you're trying to keep it a secret, you failed."

She froze, her back straightening. When she turned toward me, her face was pale, eyes wide with fear.

*What the hell?*

"Please don't tell Stefan," she pleaded.

"Why would Stefan care? Wouldn't he be happy that his brother is happy?"

"He's..." she licked her lips and took a deep breath. "Evan isn't ready to tell his brother yet. I told him we should, but he insists that he will when he's ready."

"Oh, I see." I really didn't. I just couldn't think of anything else to say. "How long has this been going on?"

Her face filled with color even as she looked down at her hands. "How long? Uh...well, about two years now."

I jerked my head back in shock. "What? You've been keeping it a secret for *two years?*"

Grace's lip quivered and I knew she was about to burst out crying. "Yes. Please, you can't say anything."

"Why the hell not? Why would Stefan care? You haven't answered me."

"We're just not ready to tell anyone. Please?"

She continued to beg me, avoiding my questions. Confused and quite frankly hurt, I nodded even though I didn't want to agree. I stood up. "I'll pass on the tea. I've gotta go," I said as I turned toward the door.

"Okay. Thanks," she whispered behind me. I didn't look back.

As I got into my car, I couldn't do anything except shake my head and wonder what the hell had just happened.

According to Stefan, him and Grace weren't even close. Perhaps that had something to do with it? Did they have a fight or something that he didn't think was important to tell me about?

Putting it in my things to discuss with Stefan later, I drove home to put the groceries away before making the visit to my mother that filled me with dread.

~*~

"Hello darling! Come in!"

My mother's cheery greeting at the door made me suspicious. I didn't let on though, choosing to smile and walk past her.

"Hi mother. I hope all is well with you."

Ugh, I hated myself at that moment. I sounded all proper and more like a friend than her only daughter.

She just smiled at me and took my arm, leading me toward the living room. "How was the trip?"

As she sat on the couch, I took a seat in a chair across from her. "It was fine."

She nodded, not saying anything else as her leg shook nervously.

I knew the feeling. I took a deep breath and leaned forward, using my knees as a rest for my elbows as I put my head in my hands.

My mother sniffled. I jerked my head up to find tears streaming down her face.

"Mom, what's wrong?"

Her eyes, so like my own, were the saddest I'd seen them since my father had left. And they were focused on me.

"You know," I stated. "But who...?"

I didn't even need to finish the question. I knew that Richard, Stefan's father, had told her.

"Can't I do anything on my own without people divulging my personal stuff before I get the chance to?"

She shook her head before glaring at me through her tears. "Why wouldn't you tell *me*, Elizabeth? What made you refuse to confide in me, when I've always been there for you?" Her voice quivered, the pain at my unintended rejection of her never more clear than in that moment. A pain I'd heard over the years and had willfully ignored. "I'd have been right by your side!"

At the sting of tears in my own eyes, I stood up and walked to the couch, sitting next to her.

"I'm sorry. I never meant to hurt you. I was just so ashamed..."

She cut me off. "Oh shush! You have *nothing* to be ashamed of!"

And for the first time since my teen years, my mother hugged me and I let her. Wrapping my arms around her, we cried together.

~*~

After a bout of crying and many tissues later, we made our way into the kitchen to have lunch. As my mother made some food, I sat at the table and enjoyed seeing the smile on her face.

I still didn't know how I would tell Stefan. Figuring my mom might have some insight, I decided to ask her. "You knew Stefan was coming to get me, didn't you?"

"The whole town knew where he was going honey," she replied, grinning. "How did it go?"

I knew my face was flushed. Even though I knew I was an adult, admitting to my mother that Stefan and I had jumped each others bones within two hours of him arriving seemed embarrassing. "You mean besides the fact he tricked me into a road trip?"

She threw her head back, laughing. The joy in it had my heart squeezing with guilt again. "It is kind of funny, *now*. But I was pretty ticked."

"Well, I'm on his side." Mom brought the salad and sandwiches over to the table and sat down. "It was long past time for you to come home. I just wish I'd done it myself."

Seeing she was getting teary eyed again, I patted her hand. "I'm here now. That's all that matters, right?"

She nodded and began eating. It was quite for a few moments until I spoke again. "He doesn't know. I…I'm supposed to tell him tonight."

"Just tell him straight up, Elizabeth. He's a good man and he loves you. How you could have ever thought otherwise is beyond me, especially since he hounded me for years to give him your number."

I shook my head. "I never thought *he* didn't love me. I just didn't love myself after that."

"In that case, always love yourself darling, even if it hurts. As long as you believe in yourself, what others believe won't matter as much, if at all."

I was the one with the watery smile then. "Thanks mom. I know he deserves the truth. He always did."

She sighed then, putting her sandwich down and covering my hand with hers. "Just remember, it's been five years and you've both probably done things that you perhaps regret or wish were different. Be open and honest. Let him be that too and be kind to yourself and to him, okay? Not everybody gets a second chance with love."

Somehow, I got the feeling there was a warning about Stefan in what she was saying. I also figured that it was all she was going to say by the fact she started eating again. Nodding, I followed suit and ate my lunch. The rest of the time passed with a comfortable silence that had me wishing I'd done this years ago.

And wondering what I'd been so afraid of. Perhaps telling Stefan wouldn't be so bad after all.

# CHAPTER FOURTEEN

The television blaring, I jumped up with a yelp as a hand landed on my shoulder. Jerking my head around, Stefan stared back at me, the grim look on his face illuminated by the overhead light.

It had gotten so late that I hadn't expected his arrival. Looking at the clock, I glared at him as I turned the television off and took a calming breath. "You scared the crap out of me! It's ten p.m. Couldn't you have at least sent me a text to let me know you were coming over?"

Not saying a word, he loosened his tie and sighed. He looked yummy. I'd never seen him dressed up in a suit before - must be something he'd picked up when he'd became a business owner - and I wanted to do nothing else but jump his bones. Pulling the tie off, he dropped it onto the couch and shrugged out of his jacket. Then, he picked up my phone, which was sitting on the side table, and handed it to me.

"I texted you about ten minutes ago," he finally responded, starting to unbutton his shirt. "It's not my fault you had the TV up so high you couldn't hear anything else."

I held up a hand, not even bothering to look at my phone. "Wait. Why are you undressing right here?"

He grimaced and removed his shirt. "I hate these suits. I'd rather be naked."

Resolving not to stare at his chest, I scowled and looked down. "What, you think you're staying the night?"

"Yes."

"How presumptuous of you."

"Really, Ellie? Are we back to that?" I could hear the weariness in his voice and suddenly felt guilty for giving him crap. "I have no reason to come here since my place is closer to town. I could have not come to see you. Would you have preferred that?"

I shook my head and he walked around the sofa. Gathering me in his arms, he sat down on the sofa and placed me so I faced him, straddling his lap.

"You promised we would talk tonight so...let's talk."

I gulped and lick my lips as my stomach knotted. "It-it's late, we could always wait until tomorrow."

His hands slid up my bare legs before gripping my thighs gently. "No, Ellie. It's time and I'm wide awake now."

Placing my hands flat against his chest, I avoided his eyes by closing mine.

*This is it, Ellie. Do it.*

"I...I didn't just get hit in the head," I finally said as his hands rubbed up and down my legs in what I assumed was supposed to be a soothing manner. "There was more."

His whole body tensed under mine as if he knew what came next, but I forged ahead before he could say anything.

"I didn't remember anything other than getting hit - I still don't. Everybody…" I took a deep breath to steady myself and keep from crying. "Nobody saw anything out of the ordinary so…I didn't get anything else but my head checked out."

"Ellie…" He lifted a hand to grip my chin and I jerked my head up to find tears filling his eyes. "You were—?"

I cut him off and jerked away, standing up. "Yes! I never meant to hurt you, dammit! Your mother, she begged and begged me to tell you when you got home, but I just couldn't do it!" I knew I was shouting now, but I didn't care. "I didn't want to face you and tell you I only knew I'd been raped because I got pregnant!"

He sucked in a breath, his eyes going wide as he spoke. "Why not? You didn't trust me?"

"No!" I shouted. "Don't you see that it never had anything to do with you, for fucks sake? I was ashamed! Somebody had done something to me while I was knocked out and I had no idea! Then to find out I was pregnant and knowing I couldn't keep—that I couldn't handle—" I couldn't even finish my sentence, the words practically choking me now.

At that he stood up and stalked toward me, grabbing my upper arms in his hands. He squeezed his eyes shut and as I saw the tear roll down his cheek, I started sobbing even harder.

"You should have told me, honey," he whispered, dragging me into his arms and hugging me tightly. "I never, *ever* would have left you if I'd known. I swear."

"I-I t-tried, I did!"

129

I really had. I'd started so many times only to end up deflecting with something that had ended up pissing him off.

He stroked my hair. "I know you did. I should have been more patient."

"Please...don't blame yourself. You...you couldn't have known."

This whole thing had my energy sapped, making me tired and weary. My head lay against his chest as he took a deep breath and sniffled.

I'd only ever seen him get emotional like this once and it had been the day he'd finally left me.

Lifting my head, I brought my hands up to wrap around his neck.

"I'm exhausted."

He didn't even say anything. And I didn't need to say another word. He picked me up and carried me to bed.

Something told me that we were gonna be all right and as I lay next to him snuggled in his arms, I slept more sound than I had in ages.

~*~

The next morning I woke up rather early.

Still wrapped in Stefan's arms, I lifted my head to look at the clock across the room.

Six thirty a.m. on the dot. On a Saturday. I wasn't shocked though because my body had gotten used to waking up this early for work these past five years.

I tried to figure out a way to slip out of his grasp without waking him. He'd thrown his leg over one of mine, with one arm around my waist and the other under my neck. It was almost our signature sleep position and amazingly, we always woke up the way we fell asleep. Well, except me, since I'd go from lying on my right side to waking up on my back.

Turning my head, I examined him. His breathing was deep and even, his mouth slightly open. I knew that if he was to wake up right now, his already dark blue eyes would be nearly black from sleep. A slow grin would make its way across his face as his hands would begin to roam my body, ready for a morning session of lovemaking that would leave me breathless.

I tried to lift his arm off my waist and it wouldn't budge. Stretching, I rolled toward him with the hope he would release me and his arms tightened instead.

Drat.

His low chuckle gave away the fact he wasn't asleep although his eyes were still closed.

"You can't leave. I've gotten used to cuddling you again while I sleep," he murmured. "Besides, you're all warm."

Using his one hand to lift my leg while inserting his leg between mine, the other grasped the back of my neck and brought my head toward his. I closed my eyes as his lips met mine before I could reply.

The kisses were slow and sleepy, making my toes curl. Other than the hand holding my leg, he wasn't touching any other part of me, my body turned on to the point of pain. His mouth made quiet love to mine, the pad of his thumb stroking my cheek lazily.

He withdrew slowly, capturing my eyes as a corner of his mouth quirked up. I was unable to look away, held hostage by the naughty glint in his. Here I laid next to him, vulnerable and exposed in a way I'd never been before. The fight I had put up hadn't been enough and he barged right back in, slowly claiming the spot in my heart that he'd always had, and more.

"What are you staring at?"

My attempt to be defensive seemed to amuse him as his smile grew wider.

"You think too much honey," he laughed. "I can practically hear your brain going."

My face heated. He slid closer to me, bringing our bodies flush against the other and resting his head on my shoulder. The soft kiss on my shoulder made me shiver. My body desired him and my heart wanted give in to him, but my head still warred with both. I knew why I fought it and I kept it to myself. I knew that surrendering to him with all of me only left me open to be hurt again. I didn't know if I could bear it.

"Stop struggling, Ellie." His voice demanded in my ear before nibbling on the lobe. "You don't have to be moving physically for me to know how you feel. I *know* you and I know how your brain works. Why are you so afraid of what we had, of what we could have now?"

He was an amazing man. I hadn't said a word, sighing in his arms as he did sweet things to me with his mouth, and yet he knew what was going on inside my head. Licking my lips, I forced myself to respond.

"I guess I'm waiting."

"Waiting for what honey? I'm here, you're here. What else do you want?"

I sighed, tears clouding my vision. "A moment I suppose. Something that will let me know I'm doing the right thing, the good thing…for me."

Silence followed my statement. I laid my hand on his arm, closing my eyes. A few seconds later, he wrapped me in his arms and squeezed tightly.

"One specific, profound moment isn't what you are supposed to spend your life looking for Ellie. Your life should include a billion different instances; ones that include all the people who matter most to you and only you."

He took a deep breath before continuing as a tear fell and slid down one of my cheeks.

"Those moments should be the ones you etch into your mind and think about - not the ones where things were bad or didn't go the way you thought they should. The only moments that matter are those that you *give* importance too."

I knew the words were true. I'd always told myself that the only thing that mattered was what I made matter to me, but I'd forgotten that. Even so, the part of me that still hung back in fear was my heart. Fragile, it made me hesitant because I didn't know if it could handle another heartbreak, no matter the source.

"You're important to me, Ellie. Hell, you are and always have been a very big part of my life. I've never loved anyone before you and if you left me for good, I'm not sure I'd love anybody after that either."

I took a steadying breath, even as my eyes still released tear after tear. "How can you say that? I pushed you away, enough to make you leave me. Why didn't you hate me for it?"

"I knew you were hurt. I didn't know why honey, but I simply couldn't watch you destroy yourself. And you wouldn't let me help you." He stroked my hair with one hand, the other still wrapped tightly around my waist. "Hating you isn't possible for me, sweetie. You're in my heart, in my head and I'm pretty sure at some point you bit me and put yourself in my blood, too."

I laughed at that and he chuckled.

"There's nobody else for me honey. And the sooner you realize that..." he trailed off with a smile.

"I know."

And I did. Yet I still couldn't say the words I knew he was aching to hear. I refused to unless I knew for sure that I meant them. When the phone rang, he answered it with a wink at me.

"What's up?"

I couldn't hear well enough to determine who the male voice belonged to, but figured it must be one of his brothers.

"Yeah, we will be there." A pause, then, "Yep, see you then."

He hung up and grinned. "Evan. Penny is inviting us over to brunch and I said we'd go. That cool?"

"Do I really have a choice?" I mock scowled at him as he chuckled, shaking his head. "Well, guess I better get dressed."

I tried to get up, but he refused to let go. Holding my chin between two fingers, he brushed a kiss against my lips and my eyes fluttered shut as I sighed. He pulled away and I opened my eyes to find him staring at me.

"Look...we need to talk later." Surprised at his statement, I frowned as my stomach twisted and he rushed ahead. "Don't make that face. I...I want to enjoy brunch with you and my family before then, okay?"

Unsure of what to say, I nodded even as the anxiety over what he might want to talk about shot through my head and my heart, unbidden and unstoppable. Then, before I could really analyze anything, he rolled over and covered me head to toe with his own body and made me forget about everything else except him.

~*~

We arrived at Penny's house, and I found myself pleasantly surprised. She lived a bit out of town, on a small road that boasted of big houses that were really far apart and each had lots of land. Last I knew, she had lived in an apartment in town.

"When did Penny move here?" I asked Stefan as we walked around the side of the brick house.

Apparently, the backyard housed the brunch - and therefore, all of Stefan's siblings. I was nervous about spending an extended amount of time with his family. They hadn't seen me since the funeral, when Yvette had accused me of putting myself in Liliana's good graces for selfish purposes.

"About a year ago, actually. She got sick of renting and began searching for something she liked. Then, this house went up for sale and she fell in love." He grinned at me and I smiled back, unable to help myself when it came to him. "So I helped her purchase it."

The gate to the backyard opened, cutting off our conversation as Penny appeared and hugged Stefan.

Turning to me, she wrapped her arms around me and squeezed until I gasped for air.

"I'm so glad you've come home, Ellie! Now Stefan will quit whining!"

I laughed as Stefan groaned beside me.

"Come in!" She stepped back. "Everybody else is here!"

Stefan grabbed my hand and interlaced our fingers before walking through the gate. I caught Penny's swiftly disguised look of surprise, replaced by a smile and a wink at me as she closed the gate and followed.

*Perhaps this won't be too bad,* I thought.

Then again, things always seemed to go downhill when around them, no matter my good intentions.

As we approached the picnic table, Evan sat in a lawn chair, while Yvette and Adrian sat on one bench. Jerome lay in the grass, staring up at the sky. Penny sat on the opposite bench as we both considered where to sit and patted the spot next to her.

"Sit here, you two," she ordered. "There's enough room for both of you."

Yvette glared at me before looking away. Stefan and I took our seats, our hands still clasped together.

"Where's brunch? I'm starving," Stefan announced, rubbing his stomach in an exaggerated manner. "I burned off a lot of calories this morning already and my breakfast wasn't big enough to make up for it."

His siblings groaned as my face heated with embarrassment. I elbowed him in the side and he grunted.

"Just trying to lighten things up," he whispered after leaning close to my ear. "They're so quiet, it's creepy."

They were. Yvette's refusal to look in my direction meant she stared away from the table in general, while Adrian looked down at his hands. Nothing new for him though as he'd always been rather anti-social. Jerome still lay on the ground not talking and Evan hadn't even looked in my direction. No doubt Grace had told him I'd seen them together the other day.

"This is depressing," I said out loud before realizing it. "Do we get music at least?"

Yvette's eyes flew to mine just as Penny laughed nervously. "You're always welcome to leave," Yvette snapped. "Nobody made you come."

I refused to let her attitude get me down. I replied with a smile, "Stefan made me actually. He tied me up until I agreed."

Yvette's eyes widened, shifting her gaze to her brother who just started chuckling.

"Knock it off, Yvette," he warned. "I want her here."

Her face flushed as she glared at me again before looking away once more.

"I'll go get the food," Penny announced, standing up abruptly and rushing away.

"Hey Evan! How's it going?" I called out, hoping to draw him over to us.

However, even after he brought his head up to look at me, he didn't really move all that much.

He shrugged. "I'm fine. Just didn't sleep that well."

Yeah, I bet he didn't. He apparently spent his nights having sex with Grace followed by sneaking out of her house in the early morning.

"Why's that? Got a girlfriend that won't let you rest?" I knew that teasing him probably wasn't a good idea but I couldn't resist. I didn't understand why they were hiding their relationship and was determined to find out.

He stiffened almost imperceptibly, his blue eyes that were so like Stefan's flying to mine.

Next to me, Stefan snickered. "Evan hasn't had a girlfriend in years. Been too busy working, he says. I don't know what he's talking about since he isn't *that* busy and we work at the same damn company."

The others laughed, with even Yvette joining in that time. Evan scowled and ducked his head. I almost felt guilty for the fact my comment caused his family to tease him. Almost. Something just wasn't right and I couldn't shake the feeling I was missing something important.

I tugged my hand from Stefan's, needing to get away for a few moments.

"I'll be right back. I need to..." I trailed off as Stefan nodded, knowing what I intended to say.

"Go through the back door and past the kitchen, it's on your right side, first door."

En route to the house, I stopped as Penny stepped out with a tray of cold cuts and cheese.

"Do you need any help?" I asked.

She shook her head and I smiled at her before stepping inside. Drying my hands on the towel a few minutes later, I exited the bathroom to head back outside. Jumping when a hand grabbed my arm as I entered the kitchen, I squealed in surprise.

"Shhhh," Evan hissed. "It's just me."

I whirled around and glared at him. "Don't fucking come up on me like that!"

His face paled even as he grimaced. "I'm sorry, I forgot."

"Too worried about saving your own ass, I assume."

He gulped and nodded. "So you do know. You won't say anything, will you?"

"No!" I huffed. "I don't get why you guys are being so weird, though. Grace says it's because you don't want to say anything. Why not?"

"You mean he hasn't told you?" Now he was scowling. "What the fuck!"

Taken aback by his response, I lifted one brow. "Told me what exactly? He said they aren't close. What am I missing?"

"He—"

Just then, Stefan burst through the kitchen door and looked straight at me.

"I've gotta go Ellie! Uh..." he saw Evan and smiled, but he couldn't hide the worry on his face. "Can you take her home man? Emergency."

Evan threw his hands up and stepped back. "No fucking way bro. I'm not touching this!"

He stalked past me and into the other room, leaving me feeling rather bewildered. Knowing that something important was going on, I forced myself to focus on Stefan and his sudden need to leave. I could get more answers later.

"What emergency?" I asked. "I'll come with you."

He rubbed his hand over his hair, letting out a deep breath before looking at me.

His phone rang again, interrupting whatever he'd been about to say. "What?"

I jumped at the bite in his tone as he answered it, but he wasn't paying attention.

"I'm on my way dammit. I can only go so fast. How do you expect me to drive if you keep call——"

The stormy look on his face on grew deeper as the person on the other end cut him off.

"You've got *no* room to talk right now," he barked into the phone. "You knew all this time and you lied to me!"

He listened for another second. I stood there, totally confused at the conversation. Who had lied to him?

"Yeah she is." Another pause then, "I said, I'm on my way. Bye!" He put his phone in his pocket and then waved at me. "All right, let's go. I'll explain on the way."

I followed him as the anxiety from earlier this morning came back full force, making me feel nauseated.

## CHAPTER FIFTEEN

The silence only lasted for a few minutes once we'd gotten into his car. Too curious to keep my mouth shut, I angled my body toward Stefan's as much as the seat belt would allow and let my questions fly free.

"Where are we going?"

"Hospital," he replied, his fingers gripping the wheel tightly. "It's not far away."

I rolled my eyes even as I took in his stiff form and clenched jaw. "I know where the hospital is. Who is hurt?"

He shifted, uncomfortable with my question but I knew he'd answer. He'd said he would and he did, unhappiness written all over his face and the tension in his body. "You remember the phone call you asked me about when I came to see you?"

"Yes."

"I've been afraid to tell you," he sighed. "I...I wasn't sure how you'd react and I wanted to get you back here before you found out. I'm still not sure, but I've got a feeling it will not be good, especially knowing what I know now."

The anxiety from earlier rose in my throat.

"Okay, so you'd always planned to tell me then?"

He nodded. "I did. I had no intentions of hiding it. I just...I had an idea of what kind of mess this would create and there's just no way to avoid it. Except I know it's much worse than I could have imagined. I've been trying to work up the nerve..."

Now it was my turn to sigh. "Just spit it out, Stefan. You've already proved how irresistible you are to me. It can't be that bad."

He laughed, and I could hear the disbelief in it. "That's the thing, honey. You are so damned unpredictable. I don't know *how* bad you will think it is. You are going to feel betrayed. And I'm sorry."

Ugh, now I really felt sick. Betrayed? Him saying sorry right off the bat? Fuck.

"Promise me something?" He placed a hand over mine. "Promise me you'll let me explain before you freak out."

Taking a deep breath and releasing it slowly, I nodded. "Okay."

Squeezing and releasing the steering wheel with his other hand a few times, he finally blew out a breath and relaxed his grip. "I have a daughter."

I snatched my hand away from his as if I'd been burned, staring at him, my eyes wide with shock. "Excuse me?" It came out as a whisper.

I wanted to jump out of the car right then. I wanted to scream and yell. But I didn't, because I'd promised him I would listen.

"I have a daughter," he repeated, the word less forceful this time. "She's at the hospital right now. She hurt herself."

"W-what...how..." I stared at him, utterly confused and yes, hurt. "Daughter? But..."

I didn't even know what to say.

Stefan gave me a sad smile as he broke the silence.

"I told you on the trip here…I did some stupid shit.
I drank, I partied, I didn't take care of myself. I
didn't sleep around though. This was…it was a one
night stand. It's not an excuse but we both got so
wasted, she came on to me and I was so hurt that I
didn't care. I took her up on it."

A low hum of anger filled my chest. I cried, unable
to stop the tears sliding silently down my cheeks. He
didn't look at me, his face red with what was no
doubt embarrassment at his confession. I didn't
understand his motivation right now, so I decided to
ask.

"Why are you bringing me here? Is this really how
you want us to meet?"

He shook his head as he pulled into a parking by
the emergency room. "That's why I asked Evan to
take you  home but since he refused, I had to bring
you with me. Just…"

Not finishing his sentence, he turned off the engine
and hopped out. I opened my door and got out before
he could come around to help, slamming the door in
my ire.

He frowned and I thought he'd say something, but
then his phone buzzed. Looking down, his hands
gripped the phone even tighter and glanced back up
at me. "I'm sorry. Just know that." He turned and
strode toward the entrance before I could reply.

I took my time following him, walking slowly,
knowing I didn't want to face his child. Nor the
mother of his child, who had no doubt been the one
on the phone he'd been snippy with. It didn't even
occur to me to ask who the woman was. All I could

focus on was him saying 'my daughter' over and over.

As I entered, I spotted him standing by the window talking to the nurse. When the door opened, he turned to look at me and held out a hand, his gaze beseeching and apologetic all at once, as if that would make this all right.

Shaking my head at him, he walked through. I tried to keep up as he presumably headed to the room his daughter had been placed in. He stopped in front of a door and turned his head, just looking at me with utter sadness on his face.

I stopped a bit further back and when he realized I wasn't going to enter with him, he went through and out of my sight.

Taking a few deep breaths, I walked toward it, the feeling of dread spreading throughout my body. It only took a second once I entered the room for the gasp to escape as I took in the child and her mother.

And Stefan standing next to his sleeping daughter, holding her hand. His eyes locked on mine and in them, the reflection of my pain.

Suddenly, every detail of the last few weeks made themselves devastatingly clear.

My heart - the part of me I'd been so close to sharing with Stefan once more - shattered as the room began to spin all around me. I must have looked funny because I saw Stefan say my name, even though I couldn't hear him through the buzzing in my head.

Then, for the first time in my life, I fainted.

~*~

I didn't want to open my eyes.

Stefan held me in his arms, which meant he must have caught me before I hit the floor. I sat on his lap, his arms wrapped lightly around my waist, my face in the crook of his shoulder. Glad he couldn't see my face, I pretended not to hear him saying my name, whispered with quiet desperation.

Good. I hope he felt absolutely wretched. I've never been very violent, but in that moment I wanted to rear back and hit him. Not only had he shared this news in the clumsiest way possible, they'd embarrassed me with their antics.

The fact it was a one night stand didn't matter.

Hell, him having a kid shouldn't upset me. Yet it had. What right did I have to be mad? I'd been gone for five years and had expected him to move on.

I knew why though. Anybody but Grace, I think I'd have been okay. But this...this whole situation pissed me off.

Not to mention the last couple weeks with Stefan were now cheapened, the moments we'd shared colored by the blatant lie he'd kept hidden from me. And Grace, couldn't forget about her part in this deception.

Steeling myself so I wouldn't cry, I opened my eyes and brought my arms up, pushing against his chest. I didn't want him touching me anymore. I just wanted to get away.

"Don't touch me!" I hissed. "Let me up, now!"

Stefan lifted his hands up and away from me in a sign of surrender. He kept his eyes on me as I scrambled up and off his lap, backing toward the doorway so I could make my escape. As, I reached it, I looked away from him and over at the bed.

Grace stared at the floor next to where Lyndsey lay sleeping. I doubt if I said her name that she'd even look at me, which I suppose was smart, since I wouldn't dare look at me either at this point if I were in her position. I'd likely say something I'd regret later.

"Are you okay?"

I whirled around at the question. Taking in his white coat, blue button up shirt and beige slacks first, I kept my eyes moving up toward his face. He was tall - if I had to take a guess, at least six-two or three, which made him taller than Stefan. Finally reaching his face, serious green eyes stared at me, concern in them. He looked at me as if he knew me, and knew what had just happened, yet I knew that couldn't possibly be true. He hadn't been living here the last time I had, so he must have moved here while I'd been gone.

He ran a hand through his short blond hair as I just stood there studying him. He cocked his head to the side, frowning as he waited for my answer.

"I-I um...yeah, I'm fine," I finally managed to stutter, feeling like an idiot.

He grinned and stepped forward. I couldn't help but notice his even, white teeth and suddenly felt very self-conscious about my appearance. If I felt icky, I could only imagine what I looked like at that moment.

"I'm Doctor Worthington. Did you hit your head?"

"Uh..." My inability to answer him made me feel even more foolish. "I don't think so."

"No, Elizabeth didn't hit her head. I caught her," Stefan chimed in, standing up.

"Good. But, if you're going to faint, a hospital is a good place to do so." He winked at me and I smiled a little, even as I felt my face heat up in embarrassment.

Was he flirting with me? I couldn't tell. I looked down and stared at his I.D.

*Simon Worthington, M.D.,* it read. And as he continued to gaze at me, I wondered who this man with the kind eyes was and where he'd come from.

Before I could speak, Grace stepped forward. "Are you here about my daughter?"

Simon cleared his throat.

"Oh, yes," he responded as he turned toward her and away from me. "Lyndsey will be fine. We stitched her up..."

I stepped out of the room as he talked to them, unable to spend one more second there. After asking a nurse for directions to the lounge, I found some vending machines and bought some water. Being in the hospital, I maintained my calm on the outside. On the inside, however, I fumed.

He told me in the car that I would feel betrayed and he'd been right.

I really didn't want to believe he had slept with Grace.

That they had a daughter.

That Grace had *hid* this from me for five fucking years.

If the woman had been anybody else, I might not have blinked at Stefan having a kid. But with Grace? I wanted to howl with the anguish I felt at knowing they had slept together.

"Uh, Elizabeth?"

I glanced up from my seat to find the doctor smiling at me.

Yep, he definitely had been flirting. He seemed kind of unsure now, which I found charming.

I didn't know what to say so I played it safe. "Doctor."

He chuckled, the sound so utterly pleasant I wanted to kiss him right there. That was a new feeling for me as I'd never been one to want to kiss complete strangers. Or men I'd just met, at least.

"Please, call me Simon," he said as he held out his hand. "I wanted to give you my card, in case...well, if you need anything."

I looked down to see the mentioned card in his hand and went to grab it with my left hand. "Oh, thanks. I...uh, I'll call you if I do."

He let go of the card but quickly grabbed my hand in his.

"Well," I saw him swallow, no doubt nervous at approaching a strange woman to ask for a date. In a hospital, at that. "I didn't notice a ring so I was wondering..."

Pleased that he wanted to ask me out as I'd suspected, I decided to make him work for it. Just for my amusement. "Wondering what? My hand is okay, I assure you. It wasn't injured in the fall."

He looked charmed with my answer, squeezing my hand a tad tighter. "It's a lovely hand." He released it and cleared his throat. "Dinner some time?"

Stefan entered the lounge then, glowering as he caught sight of me talking to the doctor. Angry at him for what he and Grace had done, and the fact he'd not told me before now, I gave in to the temptation to get back at him.

Beaming at the doctor, I nodded. "I'd love to."

"Great. Call me. I'll talk to you later." He walked past me to leave out the other door and I watched him go, deliberately avoiding Stefan's gaze.

I knew the instant Stefan stood behind me, his scent assaulting my senses. "What the hell was that, Ellie?"

"None of your business." I stood up, putting the card into my purse as I did so. "You've lost any right to question me."

He grabbed my arm and turned me toward him gently. "I know you're angry." His voice was low, intimate. "But please talk to me."

"No. I'll call a taxi. I can't be around you right now."

"Let me drive you home."

I wrenched my arm away, scowling at him. "You can stay here with your daughter and *Grace*. I'm a big girl, I can take care of myself."

With that, I stalked out of the room and didn't even bother to look back.

I'd deal with Grace later.

Right now I just wanted to get home so I could cry in private.

~*~

"Ellie, it's me again. Please stop avoiding me and talk to me. I know you're angry but I was going to tell you. I'm angry too. I didn't even know that you and Grace were still friends after all these years until you mentioned it in the car on the way here. Hell, she told me you guys weren't. I had no idea, I swear. Please call me—"

I deleted the message from my voice-mail without listening to the rest. It was Stefan's umpteenth call in the last week and I had erased every single one of them before the end. Not ready to really deal with the situation, I avoided going out unless it was to shop. Grace hadn't called me which honestly I expected. She'd have to be dumb to think I'd want to talk to her any time soon and I gave her a little credit for knowing that approaching me before I was ready would be a bad idea.

Angry and hurt, that's what I felt at that point. To be fair, I did recall the shock Stefan had tried to hide when I'd mentioned how much I looked forward to seeing Grace and Lyndsey. He wasn't lying about not knowing about our friendship, but I wasn't angry about that. My anger came from his hiding it until I'd come back to town. From not finding the time before then, in all the hours we'd spent together, to tell me before an accident had forced his hand.

And Grace. What a bitch.

All these years about how her daughter's father was a loser, a deadbeat. I'd had no reason to believe otherwise, especially since it really wasn't something you talked about more than once. I'd ask every now and then how she was doing, but Grace always said 'great!' and that had been the end of the discussion. The whole 'people will believe what they are told' had definitely been true in my case, which really didn't make me feel any better.

As for Lyndsey being his daughter, I could see it now. I knew Stefan's face like I knew my own and she was without a doubt his child. The strawberry blond hair, so similar to how Stefan's hair had been before it had darkened in puberty, the freckles across her nose, her smile. The green eyes had come from her mother, along with her slender frame. I'd always been envious of how naturally skinny Grace was.

Lost in my thoughts, I jumped when my phone rang.

With a smile at the caller ID, I answered.

"Took you long enough," I said with a chuckle, acting as if it had been days since he'd called me.

In reality, it had only been a couple hours since I'd left a message in response to his.

"What can I say? I'm a busy man," Simon quipped. "How are you?"

"I'm all right, I suppose."

"Are you serious? Just all right? You're talking to me, you should be amazing."

I laughed, which I knew was exactly what he wanted. We hadn't gone out yet due to his schedule, but we had become friends and talked every day for roughly thirty minutes, sometimes more if he had the time. I hadn't told him specifics about Stefan and me, but he knew the gist of it. We tried to avoid serious topics, instead he would tell me funny stories about work to make me laugh.

"You're right. How dare I pout when I've got some handsome man on the phone with me?"

I heard him snicker before replying.

"So, in that case, we're going on a date," he announced. "No more excuses. You've barred yourself inside for a week now. It's time to move on!"

"Simon…"

"No!" He cut me off with a laugh. "It's my day off and we're going out to dinner in the city, damn it. No need to worry about running into anybody there, right?"

"You know how I feel…"

"Yes, I know," he assured me, sighing. "It's just dinner, Elle. And until he puts a ring on it…"

He had me there. It's not like I belonged to Stefan. At this point, I wasn't even speaking to him, so why did I feel so guilty? He was the one who had messed up, not me. And a ring? If I hadn't been sure we could have a second chance at a relationship before, the chances were even more against him now.

Determined to go out and have a nice evening, I shoved aside any misgivings with the intent of building my life here once more.

"Okay," I agreed. "I'll go to dinner. Where do you want to meet?"

"Oh no! I'm coming to pick you up, like a proper date would. Be ready at five-thirty."

A glance at the clock had my eyes widening. "That's only thirty minutes from now!"

"I know and we have reservations at six-thirty so hop to it."

"Ha, ha, okay. What should I wear? Don't you need my address?"

"Dressy. And it's a small town Elle, I know where your house is."

"Right. I've been gone so long I forget what it's like to live here."

"See you in twenty-five minutes!"

With that, he hung up and I ran up the steps to get ready.

# CHAPTER SIXTEEN

The sound of the doorbell startled me.

Taking a look at my phone showed that Simon was right on time.

I always love a man who knows how to arrive on schedule. Then again, he was a doctor, his whole life no doubt revolved around them.

I ran down the steps as fast as possible in my heels, grabbing my purse and shoving my phone inside as I opened the door.

The appreciative look on his face as he took in my ensemble had me blushing.

"You look amazing Elle," he said with a smile.

I locked the handle and stepped through the door, shutting it behind me. "Thanks. You look...so normal."

He was dressed in a button up shirt and slacks, no tie. To be fair, I'd only seen him that one time at the hospital.

He laughed as he offered his arm. "This is actually pretty close to what I wear every day under the white coat, minus the tie. Shall we?"

"Oh," I didn't know what to say and felt silly. "Yes, please."

Within a few moments, we were headed toward the city.

Never one to do well with silence, I decided after a few minutes to be nosy and get to know him. "So, when did you move here?"

"About four years ago. My mother moved here two years before that to take care of her father."

"Ah. So you moved here to be closer to her then? Where did you live before?"

"Opposite coast. And I did, but don't tell her that," he said with a wink. "I just told her I wanted a slower lifestyle."

"Right." I laughed. "I'm sure she doesn't believe that."

"And you? Why did you decide to come back?"

"Why do you assume I used to live here?"

He smiled. "Everybody talks in this town. It's rare not to know everyone's stories."

"So you knew who I was in the hospital then?"

"The moment Stefan said your name, yes. And your guys' history as well."

This was a time when I truly hated being from this town. It also made me even more curious. "Why did you ask me out then, if you knew who I was and what I am to him?"

His smile grew into a full on grin and I felt the same feeling I had at the hospital. I recognized it for what it was now - desire. He was an attractive man and he knew it. He was also charming and upbeat and had learned how to utilize it effectively. I wasn't ready to acknowledge that desire out loud though.

"Because I think you're beautiful - and truth be told, I saw the hurt on your face at the hospital.

154

Believe it or not, there have been murmurs about how you'd react to finding out he had a child."

I gasped, shocked even though I knew I shouldn't be. It was a small town so of course word would get around. "Oh, I believe you. How long?"

He knew precisely what I meant. "I've known since I began working here. She had just been born and so that had started up the rumor mill. It had pretty much disappeared though, until you came back for the funeral, which is when everybody started talking about it once more."

I felt as if I'd been punched in the stomach. Knowing that people knew your business was one thing, but being talked about just made it worse. The fact it was something Stefan had done, yet I had become part of the speculation just ticked me off even more.

Simon's hand covered my own. "I didn't ask you out because I felt bad for you. I really would like to get to know you, even though I get the feeling you accepted me in the hospital just to spite Stefan," he discerned, squeezing gently.

My face burned with embarrassment at his remark. "I did," I admitted with a grimace. "But only at the hospital. Not tonight."

He lifted my hand up to his face and kissed my knuckles. My stomach clenched as he threw what could only be described as a 'hot look' my way, releasing my hand and focusing on the road once more. "I know. So let's have a nice evening out then."

I nodded even though he wasn't looking my way and tried to stay calm so I could enjoy the rest of the night with him.

~*~

We were seated quickly once we arrived. Simon ordered a bottle of the house red and I took a look at the menu.

"Never been here before, is it new?"

He'd put his elbows on the table, his chin resting on his clasped hands. "Relatively. It opened a year ago, so it's new to you."

Closing the menu, I set it down on the table. "I figured."

"Know what you want?"

I nodded, resting my hands in my lap. "I'm in a filet kind of mood."

"What? No salad and water to maintain your figure? I'm shocked!"

"No way!" I laughed as the wine arrived and poured. "I love food too much for that."

Simon lifted his glass and I followed. "I'm going to be cliche and go with 'to new beginnings'," he said before taking a sip. "Yum."

I laughed before taking a drink as he gave the waiter his order, then I gave mine and we were left alone. "So," I said with a pointed look. "Do you have any children I should know about?"

He shook his head with a chuckle. "I do not, although I wish I did. At this rate, I don't think it's going to happen."

Was he joking?

"Why not?" I couldn't resist asking.

"Age, time." He shrugged. "I've yet to find someone I want to be with who also wants a family and I'm thirty-seven. I know the risks as I get older."

"I'm sure that's rough."

"It is what it is. Then again, I'm on a date with you, so I really can't complain."

I giggled, holding out my glass even as I felt my face heat with his subtle compliment. "I think I need more wine."

He filled both of our glasses up again, our dinner arriving seconds later.

"Wow, that was fast!"

"The chef is amazing. Really, the entire staff is."

I was sure what he said was true, especially since the food tasted absolutely delicious. Eating hadn't been something I felt like doing the past week so I ate a bit slower to avoid getting sick, watching him from underneath my eyelashes. He came across as a very graceful, put together man. Alongside his charm and sense of humor, I contemplated why he was still single. Was it just his job and the hours at work that kept someone from seeing a future with him?

After my third glass of wine, I knew I'd had too much. Not having had a drink in years - with the exception of before Liliana's funeral - the wine hit me harder than it should have. I tried not to let it show as we finished up dinner.

"I was let go from my job," I shared with him, answering his earlier question from in the car. "That's why I came home. I had no reason to stay there."

"So Stefan had nothing to do with it?"

I knew I must be more than a bit tipsy if I could recognize how sober Simon was by looking at him. His face had become serious. I looked down at my hands.

"I was planning to come back anyway. I had no reason to stay there any longer. He just brought me back sooner. He—He really wanted to try again, he said, but I wasn't sure. Hell I'm still not sure, especially now."

He inclined his head in acknowledgment. "I understand. So whats your plans then? Looking for work?"

I shrugged as I looked back up at him. "I didn't really have a plan. Everything has happened so fast..."

The waiter put the bill on the table and without taking his eyes off me, Simon put his card into the holder and handed it back with a 'thank you'.

Putting his hand over mine, he caught my eyes with his. "Are you okay?"

I couldn't help but giggle, which gave me away. "Why do you ask?"

"You've got a slightly unfocused look on your face, that's why. How long has it been since you drank?"

I hiccuped then, which just made me laugh harder.

Simon stood up and came around to me, pulling me up from my chair as the waiter arrived back at the table.

Seconds later, we were outside the restaurant walking toward the car. I stopped abruptly and Simon looked at me with one brow raised. "What is it?"

I turned left and then right, staring up at the buildings. "What street are we on?"

"Why?"

"A year, you said a year! What used to be here?"

He must have heard the sudden panic in my voice, his grip tightening on my arm.

I looked up into his eyes and saw exactly what I feared. This building used to be the club, but I hadn't recognized it because of the new buildings surrounding it and the new decor inside.

"Fuck," he swore. "I'm sorry, I should have...Get in the car Elle, come on."

That's when I heard his voice. I stiffened and jerked my head to the left, only to see Lawrence stepping out of his car while on his cell phone. He hung up as he started to walk across the street. Seeing us standing there, he tipped his hat, no recognition in his eyes as he entered the restaurant.

*It was him. He'd done it.*

My brain shouted at me, my body suddenly cold, sober.

"Elle? What's wrong?"

"I..." Not sure what to say to a man who didn't even know the whole story, I turned toward the car. "Nothing, let's go."

Simon looked as if he wanted to say something, but decided against it.

Moments later, we were headed home in total silence.

~*~

"I suppose what happened to me was known enough for you to find out too?" We had just arrived back at my place.

Simon turned the engine off and turned to face me. "I know the basics. I have a feeling that wasn't it though - not by the way you stiffened when you saw that man."

159

I wanted to puke, that's how sick I felt in that moment. "I don't know that it was him. I don't remember anything."

I watched as his expression clouded in anger. "Your mind remembered, even if you don't know the specifics. Something clicked."

A tear slid down my cheek and I swiped it away. "It doesn't matter anymore. I don't think he recognized me. There is no proof."

"Are you fucking serious? Of course it matters!" Then he paused, frowning. "What do you mean there is no proof? Proof of what?"

I hadn't meant to say that. I didn't want to discuss this, feeling sicker by the second. I grabbed the handle and opened the door. "I have to go."

"Elle. Stop." I paused but didn't look at him and he sighed. "Let me walk you to your door."

"I'm fine," I protested, even as he closed his door and came around to mine. "I can do it by myself."

"Even if that's true, you were tipsy enough at the restaurant to require assistance." He took my arm with his and shut the door. "I won't let you fall, Elle. You are really upset. You can talk to me you know."

I continued to say nothing as we walked up the steps and stopped. Digging for my keys, I became frustrated when I couldn't find them thanks to the tears blurring my eyes. Simon grabbed my purse.

"Let me help." He rummaged around for a few seconds in the dark.

"I don't know why the porch light hasn't come on," I mumbled and he chuckled as he pulled my keys out.

"Don't worry, I'm good at feeling for things in the dark."

The joke caught me unawares and made me laugh, which then turned into a sob.

"Damn it," Simon said as he pulled me into his arms. "Wrong time to try and be funny."

"I'm s-sorry—"

"Don't be. Let's get you inside."

He released me and using his cell for light - why hadn't I thought of that? - slid the key home, opening the door.

"Which way to your room?" He asked as we stepped in and he shut us inside.

"Uh...up the steps to the right."

"Do you need anything from down here?"

I shook my head and he guided me up the steps, one hand on my elbow.

With his solid grip and softly spoken questions, I got the impression he was in doctor mode now, making sure I made it safely to bed so I didn't hurt myself. The thought made me smile.

"You're sweet," I announced rather loudly and winced. "Pfft...I guess I'm a lightweight."

He led me to the bed, where I promptly fell forward on it.

I heard him chuckle as he sat down on the bed. "Do you need anything? Or for me to call someone, perhaps to come over here so you won't be alone?"

I lifted my head but just barely, turning to look at him only to find myself staring at his leg. "Uh...aren't you here? I'm not alone."

"I can't stay, Elle. You probably won't even remember this in the morning. How you got so drunk off of three glasses is amusing, though."

I blew a piece of hair out of my face, lifting myself up on my elbows. My brain was definitely muddled.

I didn't understand why he couldn't stay. "Why not?"

Oh god, had my voice quivered? I think so.

He reached out, tucking a piece of hair behind my ear, not saying a word.

Tears clouded my vision. "I've ruined our date haven't I?"

Why did I care? I hadn't wanted to go out with him really, had I? It was just meant to piss off Stefan…but then I started to like him. Crap, when had that happened?

His face fell. "No," he replied sharply. "*You* didn't do anything wrong, Elle. I don't need you to tell me what happened, I put it together myself. You've every right to be upset. I'm not rejecting you."

The tears came harder at his words, at his discovery and the next thing I knew, I was lying next to him in bed, cradled in his arms.

I don't know how long I cried, but he just held me, stroking my hair, silent.

When morning came, he was gone and I had no idea of when I'd fallen asleep.

# CHAPTER SEVENTEEN

As luck would have it, I didn't have a hangover. Thanking the stars for that, I changed clothes and headed downstairs.

My purse was right by the door on the table and I searched through until I found my phone. Seeing it was dead, I put in the charger before heading out the door to go grocery shopping. I'd just text Simon when I got back in.

I arrived at the store minutes later, which was near empty due to the early hour, as always. The lone cashier smiled as I walked by and I smiled back at her.

Strolling through the aisles, I had nearly finished shopping when I ran into Penny.

"Oh, hi Elizabeth!"

I'd always liked Penny. She and I shared a similar sense of humor, along with being shy and introverted.

"Hey Penny. How are you?"

"You're asking about me?" Her mouth had rounded in an 'o' of surprise. "It's me who has been worried about you!"

I gave her a small smile. "I guess you heard."

She rolled her eyes. "My brother is a dingbat. I'm sorry I didn't tell you myself, I really should have instead of listening to his promises that he would. We all thought you knew when you came to brunch..."

I shrugged. "It's okay. I think he should have told me himself too. It was his place, not anybody else's."

At that, her face lit up. "You wanna do something some time? I know you don't have many friends, but I consider you my friend."

"Did Stefan...?" I couldn't even finish the question.

She nodded, her eyes going soft with sympathy. "He didn't give specifics, he just said there was more to it. We understand everything. How anyone could be mad at you for that would be beyond my understanding!"

"Thanks, Penny. I'd like that. I'll call you later okay?"

"Sure!" She gave me a hug before heading off in the other direction.

I just sighed in relief that I hadn't run into Stefan instead and finished shopping.

However, as I pulled up in the driveway, I realize I'd spoken too soon. Stefan was sitting on the front porch and lifted his head from his hands as I got out and shut the car door.

"What did you plan to do, sit there all day until I got back?"

"If I had to, yes."

I crossed my arms over my chest, standing a few feet away from him, scowling. Afraid he would touch me, afraid he wouldn't. Still angry, still hurt yet desiring him so much it hurt. I wanted to hate him for hurting me as much as I wanted him to just take me in his arms. I fisted my hands, my nails biting into my skin in order to keep from touching him.

He looked like shit, his red eyes giving away the fact he probably hadn't slept well in days. At least he knew how I felt, although I'd slept really well last night for the first time in a week.

I turned and went to my trunk, pulling out my groceries. Stefan showed up beside me and pulled out the rest before closing the lid.

"Uh, thanks."

We were inside and heading to the kitchen before he spoke again. "I'm an idiot."

"Duh." I started putting the groceries away, making sure to avoid looking at him or being near him. He stood near the door, not really daring to come inside, his hands shoved in his jean pockets.

"I wasn't sure you were getting my messages."

*Slam, slam, slam.*

The cans of tomato sauce hit the counter as I put them down with more force than necessary. I heard him sigh and smiled to myself.

"How many times am I going to have to apologize, Ellie?"

At that I turned around, glaring at him. "As many times as it takes, Stefan, and then perhaps some more. What you and her did was inconsiderate. How *you* finally had to tell me was just fucking ridiculous. You should have told me *before* you were forced to!"

He flinched, his face reddening at my reprimand.

"You shouldn't have come here. I'm not ready to even consider forgiving you, let alone talk with you like a civil person."

His expression clouded as his jaw tensed. "What you meant to say is that you obviously can't be that hurt since you already went on a date with what's his name."

"Considering you went and fucked *what's her name* in no time after I left, you can't really talk can you?"

He stormed toward me, his fists clenched. "You slept with him?"

I laughed at the incredulity in his voice. "His *name* is Simon and it's none of your business!"

"In that case, her name is Grace and it's not any of your business!"

With that, I slapped him.

As his hand flew up to his cheek and mine covered my mouth, he laughed.

Laughed.

"Feel better, honey?"

I pointed toward the door. "Get out."

He put a hand on either side of me, trapping me against the counter. "Not a chance," he whispered, our faces so close now that our noses nearly touched. "Do it again."

What? He wanted me to hit him again?

He must have seen the question on my face, his smile growing wider. "Yep, do it. Hit me, if it will make you feel better, heal the hurt. I'm just warning you though, it won't."

My shoulders sagged as I sighed. "No, you're right, it won't. So please leave."

"I can leave your house Ellie, but its kinda hard to just push me out of your heart isn't it? Not so easy. And its not easy for me to just let you go. I don't want to give up, or for you to give up. I'm sorry, I

166

should've told you right away. We can't work this out if you won't talk to me."

Refusing to cry, I closed my eyes and childish as it was, covered my ears with my hands. "Go away, damn you! Haven't you done enough. Leave me alone!"

It only worked to muffle his words, not block them out completely.

"Ellie...you can block your ears to what I have to say, and you can close your eyes to avoid seeing me, but you can't keep your heart from loving me. In one instant, I did something that forever changed my life, but how long will you punish me for it? I get it, you're angry. You're hurt. Be angry. Be hurt. Date that guy if you must. But you know where to find me honey and you can be damned sure I'll be waiting for the moment you're in my arms again. Because you will be. We belong together and you know it."

I opened my eyes to glare at him, unblocking my ears to shove him away with my arms and he stepped back. "I'm not punishing you for what you did then. I'm not even punishing you now. You did this to yourself when you didn't have the guts to tell me in private, before you took me to that hospital. Now get out."

He didn't say anything else, just leaned in and kissed my forehead before turning around and walking out.

~*~

"Do you think you're punishing him for then or now? Or both?"

Simon and I were sitting on my love-seat, our knees touching as we faced each other. It had been near ten when he'd finally gotten off work and called me to see how I was. Embarrassed over the night before, I invited him over and he offered to bring food. Then, we'd talked about our day and now here we were, talking about Stefan.

I put the container of sweet and sour chicken down, sighing. "I admit, I'm hurt over the fact it was her. Out of everybody, he had a child with her. I don't want to be angry about it. I have no right, but I am."

He put his down as well and scooted over, putting his arm along the head of the sofa behind my head. "I don't think you necessarily have *no right*. After all, she was your best friend and continued to act the same all these years, holding back vital information from you."

I leaned my head back and closed my eyes. "True. I've yet to talk to her about all of this and I'm not sure I ever want to."

"While Grace might deserve that, her daughter doesn't. She knows you as her aunt, doesn't she?"

"How do you know that?"

"At the hospital, she mentioned you. How she was having her party and she was finally going to meet her aunt Elizabeth in person. She went on and on about it, much to Grace's embarrassment. I gathered that much."

I groaned, covering my eyes with one arm. "I totally forgot about her party! They'll both be there, I'm not sure I can handle it on my own."

"What about bringing me? Or would that be too weird?"

I turned my heads toward him, my mouth falling open before I snapped it shut. "Are you serious? Bringing you is like…" I paused, searching for the right words. "They're practically my family. It'd be like announcing that we're dating to them."

His free hand slid under the one on my lap, threading our fingers together as he leaned closer. "Hmm, dating." He looked up at the ceiling for a moment before meeting my eyes with his. "Is that dating as in, going on dates but not actually being a couple, or is that the boyfriend and girlfriend type of dating?"

I knew the mischievous grin on his face meant he understood exactly what type I referred to, but he wanted me to say it.

His mouth was inches from mine and I wanted him to kiss me. I wouldn't make the first move though. At least then, if we kissed, I could say I wasn't the one who had initiated it. I still felt guilty for liking him so soon after things happened with Stefan and wasn't sure where to go from here.

I licked my lips, his eyes darkening as they dropped down to gaze there. "It would be a serious declaration," I whispered, my mouth suddenly dry. "You've no idea the kind of questioning you'd get from them."

He laughed, the sound low and sexy, then lightly kissed my cheek. "Wanna play a game?"

"What kind of game?" We were both barely speaking now, the words spoken on a breath of air.

"Simon says."

My eyes jerked up to his, even as the deliciously devilish grin spread across his face.

"The rules are, you do what I say, as long as I say 'Simon says' - I'm sure you remember this game, don't you?"

"But—"

He put one finger over my mouth. "Simon says you aren't allowed to talk unless I tell you to."

I scowled at him but remained quiet, the idea of playing the game oddly appealing as it made my stomach clench.

"Now," he said as he removed his finger. "Simon says to ask me to go with you to the party."

I didn't know whether to be amused or turned on at the way he commanded me with this game. Amused, I played along.

"Simon, will you go to this party with me?"

His eyes practically danced with amusement. "Yes, I would be honored."

Removing his hand from mine, it skimmed up my leg and to my waist. His hand stopped there, resting lightly. "Now, Simon says you have to kiss me." His hand tightened on my midsection as I opened my mouth to protest. "Ah ah, you know the rules. You have to do what Simon says. And I know you want to. But if you don't kiss me, I can't know that you actually like me."

I gulped even as he just sat completely still, watching me.

"It's just a kiss, Elle," he reassured me. "You may think I kiss like a frog, but you can't know if you don't try."

"I'm not sure…"

"Our lips are inches apart, you've only got to barely move forward—"

I brought my hands up to his shoulders, stopping him in mid-sentence and smiled as his eyes widened.

Then it dawned on me. Simon wasn't sure I liked him romantically and didn't want to be the first one to make a move.

"Simon didn't say—"

"Simon should shut up," I advised as I slid my arms around his neck and touched his lips with mine.

He smiled against my mouth, his arms circling my waist, enclosing my body inside of them.

My first thought was that it was entirely different than when Stefan and I were together.

With him, kissing and touching was explosive, like a passion neither of us could control. It started out as instant hotness, our bodies aching to be together as quick as possible. Our fervor matched his temper in its fierceness, it's refusal to be denied no matter what lay between us.

The feeling with Simon was similar to turning the heat on and having it slowly warm up the room, or a blaze started in the fireplace that slowly builds up until the flames are so high they are licking the chimney. Soon, I knew I would be aching to touch that fire, no matter if it burned me because it was just that irresistible.

I wiggled to get closer and seeming to recognize what I wanted, he pulled me onto his lap so I straddled him. His hands didn't stray from around my waist though and I sighed into his mouth as I pulled away enough to speak.

"Touch me."

His arms tightened around me and I felt him flexing his hands, gripping the back of my shirt almost desperately.

"I can't," he ground out. "If I do that, I won't be able to stop and I'm not that kind of man."

I froze and looked him straight in the eye, lifting a brow. "Not the kind of man...to what? Have sex with the girl he 'Simon said' into becoming his girlfriend?"

He grinned even as his face reddened. "Uh...well," he swallowed and I felt my mouth drop open. "Yes."

"You aren't saying what I think you're saying are you?"

I'd give it to him, he was brave. His eyes never strayed from mine as he nodded.

Handsome, funny and kind Doctor Simon was a thirty-seven year old never married virgin.

Oh boy.

# CHAPTER EIGHTEEN

I started to get up off his lap, feeling awkward all of a sudden.

"No," he objected, tugging me back down. "Please stay."

"How—what—" I didn't know what to say, or what to do with my hands. I finally decided to place them back on his shoulders, which seemed innocuous enough. I sat very still, almost statue-like.

"Relax, Elle," he said soothingly, gliding his hands up and down my sides. "You can't catch it."

I tried to suppress a giggle and failed.

Then he started laughing and I let out a breath, my body softening. "Okay now that we have that awkwardness out of the way, I can explain if you want."

Hearing the restraint in his voice, I could only guess at the depths of his self-control when it came to his obvious self-imposed virginity. Tilting my head to the side, I admired him with what I hoped was a calm demeanor. "Yes, I do."

His mouth quirked in amusement at me, but he glanced away, as if suddenly lost in thought.

173

"My father was a horrible womanizer. My parents used to fight all the time and when I was ten, my mother got fed up and divorced him. I later found out that he'd pretty much cheated on her their whole marriage, and even beforehand. This was later though. He demonstrated his ways to me when I'd go visit him and it seemed like every other week, he'd have a new girlfriend over while it was his time with me.

"So many of them were just with him for his money, others actually started out thinking he was a great human being until he dumped them within weeks of meeting them. I was disgusted by his behavior but visiting seemed like the 'right' thing to do. Eventually though, I got to the age where I became so busy that I used school and other things as an excuse not to visit. I also became very determined not to become him.

"In order to keep my promise, I stayed single all through high school, then college although that was more because I was too busy preparing for med school. Got into medical school and wanted to do really well, plus not stress anyone else out with my schedule. By the time residency ended, I had hit thirty and started working.

"I finally started going on dates, but none of them ever went anywhere. One thing or another would prevent us from going out, or they'd find someone who could give them more of their time, etcetera. Then I moved here and until I met you, I'd only been on two dates, both with women who never called me again."

He sucked in a breath as he looked back at me.

Me, I was blown away by his explanation. Here was a man who respected women, so much he avoided involving himself with them for years as to not feel like he was using them in the same manner his father had, and wanted nothing more than to have a relationship that ended up with having a family.

In that moment, I fell in love with Simon just a little.

And promptly doubled my troubles.

"I've rendered you speechless."

"Ah..." I cleared my throat, finding it hard to form my thoughts into words. "No. I just...what to say? That whole explanation was...so much sexier than you intended it to be I think."

His hands, which had fallen to my thighs, bit into them at my words. "And just why is my self-imposed sexual exile sexy?"

I moved, bringing our bodies as close to one another as possible, less than an inch apart from our lips to our stomachs. As close as two people could be while dressed, I wrapped my arms around his neck and rolled my hips almost imperceptibly. A groan fell from his lips even as his hands clutched my hips, holding me still.

I moved to rest my head in the crook of his shoulder, sighing. "It just is. It's unexpected and well, hard to explain, but I think you exhibited a self-control any person would be proud to call their own."

"From my current position, it seems like making me lose control would please you," he growled.

I wiggled for good measure, giggling as he swore. Then, I lifted my head and found his hot, needy gaze locked on me.

"I should go," he said with a frown. "I need to get to bed."

Looking up at the clock, I was shocked to discover just how late it was. "You're too late, Cinderella," I teased him, laughing. "It's midnight and you'll turn into a pumpkin any minute now."

He snickered, even as his hands toyed with the hem of my shirt, wanting to explore yet hesitant.

I arched a little and one slipped under my top, the heat of his skin against mine causing me to gasp and his control to crack just a little.

Finding this as sensual as I did aroused me like nothing else ever had. Knowing that he hadn't touch anybody else in a similar way, the reverence in his soft, nervous caresses had me curving into him again, desiring the stroke of his hand elsewhere.

"Elle..." he breathed my name, trailing off as his free hand found the back of my neck and tugged our faces closer. "Kiss me goodbye."

Simon's soft plea was swallowed up in our mouths meeting again, tongues mating lazy and slow as he moaned, rocking us together all on his own this time. My hands slid up into his hair, guiding him almost as much as he guided me. For a few moments, I wondered if this would go on forever and part of me hoped it would.

Yet when his hand roamed around front and found my breast, he pulled it away as if scalded, disconnecting our lips as well. Gently lifting me off his lap, he placed me next to him before standing up. Running a hand through his already mussed hair, he stood facing away from me as he spoke.

"I'll call you after my shift, okay?"

"Uh...yeah, sure."

He didn't say anything else as he headed out of the room. Then, he tossed a grin over his shoulder just before turning the corner. A moment after the door shut quietly behind him, I flopped back onto the couch and burst into laughter, feeling so joyous I just had to let it out.

~*~

Penny invited me out to lunch on Wednesday.

As we continued to sit in the diner after finishing our food, I checked my phone for what seemed like the millionth time.

"Ya know looking at it repeatedly won't make him send you a message any faster right?"

I blushed, putting down my phone and sitting back. I knew she was right, even though it had been three days since I'd seen Simon. We had talked and he said that perhaps we'd see each other this evening but so far, no message from him.

"You're right. I guess I'm just nervous because it's been so long since I actually dated anyone." Stefan didn't count, we'd just been having sex but I wouldn't tell his sister that.

Her eyebrow rose even as she smiled. "How long? You didn't date anyone while you were gone?"

"I did once. A few weeks and it was a huge mistake."

She laughed, leaning forward. "You're being silly Elizabeth. He spends all his free time talking to you and so far, his days off with you. From what you've said, he's also totally into you."

"I know," I said with a sigh. "I just don't want to mess things up. I seem to be good at it."

"Bull. Chill out and relax."

I stuck my tongue out at her, crossing my arms over my chest. "Fine, fine." I decided to change the topic. "So, where is this party going to be exactly?"

"My house, actually," she replied with a grin. "Although that wasn't the plan at first, I insisted."

"Oh? Why?"

"Because then I can invite anybody I want."

"Nice!"

"Yep. Which means you can bring Simon and nobody will say a word to you. Well, they better not."

My eyes watered at her kindness and I groaned, putting my face into my hands. "I'm sorry, don't mind me. I'm such a sap lately."

"Its okay," I heard her say a little lower. "A lot has happened."

I peeked at her through my fingers. "Seems you're the only one who sees it that way. I'm surprised you aren't rooting for your brother."

"Oh, a part of me is," she admitted. "I'm a loyal sister that way. But I also think what he did was wrong and I've told him so many times."

Since I agreed with her, all I could do was nod. "Is Yvette dancing on tables in her happiness yet?"

At that, Penny snorted.

"Honestly, I think that girl is insane. I love her, she's my sister, but sometimes I wanna smack her upside the head."

Now I was the one grinning. "Me too!"

Just then, my phone buzzed, making us both jump.

"Really! We've been waiting and it shocks us!" Penny threw her hands up. "Be right back, going to the bathroom."

She took off and I picked up my phone, where a message from Simon awaited me.

*'Sorry no text earlier, busy day. Miss you (can I say that yet?). Dinner at my place, six?'*

Seeing the 'miss you' sent a rush of affection through me, his 'can I say that yet' an adorable question a man well versed in dating would have never asked, which only made it all that more sweet. As Penny came back toward the table, I typed what I hoped was an equally pleasant response.

*'No worries, lunch with a friend. Me too (yeah, you can if I can). Dinner sounds good, address? Looking forward to it. Should I dress up or is this a clothing optional dinner? xo'*

I hit send just as she sat down and her pursed her lips, gazing at me expectedly.

"Dinner at his place."

She let out a squeal, making some heads turn our way.

"Geeze girl, calm down. It's not like we're gonna have sex."

Her mouth rounded as my phone buzzed in my hands and I looked down, only to feel my face heat at his words.

*'Doesn't matter, would want you in anything I'm sure. Cant wait, my address is...—-'*

Penny snatched the phone out of my hand to read it, then glared at me. "Not gonna have sex? That's not what it sounds like to me with 'would want you in anything' *at all*."

It wouldn't be appropriate to tell her Simon's secret, so I said the first thing that came to mind. "Ugh," I rolled my eyes, grimacing as I took my phone back. "It's not been long since I was with your brother, Penny. It's too soon."

"Yuck! I know I am twenty-seven but I still don't want to imagine my brother having sex!"

I snickered at her childish response. "What, you've never had sex?"

She busted out laughing. "Are you kidding me? I've dated, and had sex. Not that I'd share that with my brother, he gives most men a dirty look."

"Yeah, that's cuz he knows what men are like." *Like himself, especially.* I didn't say that out loud. "Are you dating anyone now?"

The beautiful flush crossing her face, along with the sudden dreaminess in her eyes, told me all I needed to know.

"I'm not ready to tell anyone," she hissed. "It's only been a few months."

"Hey, your secret is safe with me. Heaven knows I have enough of them already, it's just one more."

"Ooh tell me!"

I shook my head and she leaned in.

"Anybody I know?"

"Who do you know that I don't know?"

"Good point."

With that, we laughed and left the diner, parting ways after she made me promised to bring Simon by before the party.

~*~

I pressed the doorbell to Simon's place at five minutes until six.

Within seconds the door swung open, where I found myself staring at his wet, bare chest. Taking in his broad shoulders, which his clothing had only hinted at, my eyes instantly traveled down his surprisingly toned body, only to discover his lower half wrapped in a towel. Snapping my head up, he stared at me with an unrepentant grin.

"Are you going to come in or just stand there admiring me?"

Feeling brazen, I stepped inside only to bring my body flush against his, my gaze holding his.

At his sudden intake of breath, I put one hand on his chest and slid it down slowly. "So, by the way you greeted me, I take it that I should have arrived in nothing but an overcoat."

He captured my hand before it reached the towel, holding it in place as his eyes darkened at my comment with a desire he couldn't hide, his body tensing.

"I just stepped out of a quick shower and didn't want to keep you waiting too long," he murmured, the low timbre filled with a need he adamantly denied. "Let me put some clothes on real fast."

I hooked my other arm around his neck and stood on tip toe, kissing the side of his mouth. His free arm wrapped around my waist as he moaned, the other reflexively squeezing our hands that were already connected. I moved down his jaw slowly, each successive peck causing his breathing to quicken and his hand to clench and unclench my blouse. His eyes had closed and I smiled to myself before moving back to his mouth, my mouth just shy of touching his.

"Have you ever let a woman touch *you*, Simon?"

He shook his head, yet didn't move to disconnect from me.

Taking that as permission, I slid my hand up and into his silky hair, bringing our lips in contact on an exhale.

Never one to be in charge before, I found my sudden control to be a high, near ecstasy. To have such a big and strong man at my mercy was a heady sensation. Applying a bit of pressure, his mouth opened under mine and my tongue swept in, only to find his ready and willing to battle. His hand released mine, coming up to cup my jaw as the other slid down and cupped my ass, moaning into my mouth.

With that small surrender, every thought aside from getting closer fled from my mind. I didn't think of my problems, of what Stefan and Grace had done, of where my life was going. The only thing on my mind became touching, kissing and exploring Simon; everything else didn't matter and I didn't want to care.

I took the opportunity to explore again, my nails lightly scraping down until they met the towel, then around his side, to up and down his back. His grip tightened, his hunger unleashed more by the second, the war our tongues waged sending shocks of pleasure through me.

My body was on fire now and he had become the only one able of putting it out.

When he ripped his mouth away from mine, I couldn't prevent the sob of disappointment from escaping.

"We've got to stop," he rasped, gritting his teeth even though his hold on me didn't lessen. "If we don't..."

"Don't," I said without opening my eyes. It came out soft, a whisper in the air because the ability to do more than breathe was beyond me at this point. "Please don't stop."

He swore, his hand releasing my behind only to slide under my skirt to grab my bare cheek with a firm grip. "No panties? You're going to be the death of me!"

I nipped his chin, a naughty smirk on my face. "At least you wouldn't die a virgin," I countered. "Now *that* would be a really bad shame."

With that, he threw his head back and laughed.

I was literally engrossed by the beauty of it, the sound deep and full. It sent a thrill through me, which I felt all the way to the tips of my toes. His neck was bared and before I could even think about not doing it, I arched up and nipped him near the base.

He hissed, whirling me around before I could blink and backing me up against the wall. His mouth covered mine, hungry in its search for entrance which I granted, incapable of denying him anything at this point. Not that I could even if I wanted to.

I moaned, the sound lost as he angled his head to go even deeper, rocking us together gently. I could feel him against where I wanted him most, unable to do anything about it. I thrust my hips and he tightened his hold on me, plundering my mouth with a ferocity I didn't know he had.

Then, suddenly, he was gone.

I slapped my hands against the wall to steady myself as he stepped back. Pleased to see him breathing heavily, my own gulps of air fit right in.

"I'm..." he cleared his throat, swallowing rapidly. "Need to...um, get dressed. Yes, that. I'll be right back."

C.S. Janey

Too stunned to speak, I just stared as he turned and
bolted up the steps.

# CHAPTER NINETEEN

"We can cuddle during the movie if you don't tempt me."

We were sitting on his sofa after dinner. Dark except for the light off the television, we sat next to each other with me leaning into Simon, his arm around me.

"You're the one who came to the door practically naked. I'm only human."

"I've gotta move a bit slower, I think," he spoke softly. "I'd like to just lie here with you. Think we can do it and keep our clothes on?"

It had been a good ten minutes before he'd come back dressed earlier. He'd thrown on a pair of khaki shorts and an open short-sleeved button up, which had only made me want to touch him again. Sitting next to him brought its own special form of torture, in that he smelled like sunshine, although I knew that had to be his detergent. I wanted to tell him that thirty-seven years was probably slow enough, but I refrained.

"I'll behave if you do," I promised instead, standing up.

He grabbed a throw pillow, placing it under his head as he stretched out on the sofa, smiling up at me.

"You're taking up all the room!"

He clasped my hand and pulled me down until I was on top of him. I moved a little and got comfortable, then he wrapped his arms around me. His chin rested on the crown of my head and he sighed.

"This is...so nice," he murmured with a yawn.

"Mmhmm."

As the movie began, one of his hand caressed my arm and across my back. The repetitive motion had me feeling drowsy, my eyes drifting shut as I just enjoyed being close to him. I couldn't remember the last time Stefan and I had just lain together, enjoying the company of the other without having sex first. Probably before everything had gone so wrong.

When his arm stopped a little while later, I felt their heaviness against my back and knew he'd fallen asleep. Attempting to get up to leave, his eyelids drifted open as he smiled sleepily.

"No. Stay," he murmured drowsily. "So...nice..."

Really not wanting to leave anyway, I kissed his jaw before resting my head against him once more.

The next thing I knew, Simon was whispering in my ear.

"Elle? It's time to get up."

I lifted my head and opened my eyes to find that not only I was no longer lying on him, but we were in a bed.

"How?"

His eyebrows rose, his face serious. "Magic."

I groaned and rolled to my side, at which point he decided to pull me toward him and his bare chest.

"I carried you here, of course. You were snoring a little, was cute."

"Oh! Don't tell me that!" I hid my face in my hands.

He chuckled, his hands rubbing up and down my back as he nuzzled my neck.

"What time is it?"

"Six," he mumbled, pressing a hot kiss to my shoulder. "I have to leave for work soon."

"Damn. So you're working me up for nothin'?"

"You're right, I shouldn't..."

"I'm kidding!" I cut him off, sliding my hands up to put my arms around his neck. "Who knows when I'll see you again, have to take what I can get."

He looked at me then, sliding a hand up to the back of my neck, his eyes serious.

"It's different than I expected."

Confused, I frowned.

"What is?"

His eyes dropped my mouth.

"Waking up next to a woman."

I gasped. "Seriously? I could see the no sex thing but not even sleeping next to anyone in all this time?"

He tugged me closer, making it very clear how turned on he was, his eyes deepening in color. "My first thought," he said with a quick peck on my lips, ignoring my question. "Was how absolutely beautiful you looked while asleep. I didn't want to disturb you."

"What was your second?" I asked, unable to look away.

"That I wished you were naked, so I could see how much better reality is than my imagination."

"Did you steal that line from a movie?"

"Why? It is cheesy?" He grimaced. "Maybe that explains it, all these years I used terrible lines..."

I cut him off with a soft kiss, only to end up beneath him as he covered my body with his.

After several moments, he lifted his head and smiled before rolling away, tossing the blankets aside as he sat on the edge of the bed.

"All right, time to get dressed," he said, running a hand through his hair. "Otherwise I'll be late!"

It wasn't until I sat up on my elbows that I realized he'd been completely naked this entire time and got a nice view of his toned backside as he stood up and walked away.

~*~

The closer to the party it got, the more nervous I became.

Especially since Penny had sent me a text the day after I'd spent the night at Simon's, informing me that the party had been moved up a week. Grace had called her in a panic, explaining that Stefan and Evan would have to go out of town on the original date and needed to have it happen sooner.

Now it was Tuesday and the party was this upcoming Sunday.

It was also Simon's first day off since we'd seen each other last and we were walking downtown, hand in hand.

"You doing okay?"

His voice invaded my thoughts and I jumped.

"Huh? Yeah, I'm fine. Why?"

"You haven't really mentioned what happened on our first date. I've been afraid to ask but the look on your face had me wondering enough just now to ask anyway."

Ah, he thought my anxiety was over seeing Lawrence.

I shrugged. "I haven't really thought about it, which is odd because my brain shouted at me that it was him, but I feel so glad that I can't remember. I dealt with a lot of my issues about it in therapy."

I truly hadn't. However, I certainly wasn't going to be near that restaurant any time soon, perhaps ever again, but I'm sure he'd gathered that.

He nodded, bringing up our clasped hands to kiss the back of mine. "If you need to talk about it, I've always got an open ear, all right?"

I beamed up at him in answer, just as we entered the local diner for some lunch.

Only to have Grace literally bump right into Simon.

He used his free hand to steady her, her face flaming as she noticed me standing next to him.

"S-sorry!" She stuttered, twisting her hands together. "I looked down for just a second—"

"No problem," Simon said smoothly. "How is Lyndsey?"

Grace's face lit up, making my heart twist in a bitter emotion I didn't want to examine. "She's fine, her arm is fine. She's gonna have a scar now to show off which is all she talks about. Kids!"

"Yep, she'll no doubt get lots of attention if she wants it," he replied with a laugh. "Can't wait to have my own children one day."

At that, Grace smile softened but she kept her gaze focused on Simon. I silently fumed. "Never knew such joy in my life, truly." She looked down at her watch. "I'd love to stay and chat but I gotta go!"

He nodded as she threw me an unsure glance before walking out. "Awkward," Simon muttered, guiding me to a booth near the back.

I didn't even bother to respond, his summary of the occurrence spot on.

Sitting in the back was a good choice, because people would be less likely to walk back here to talk to him, as they often did when we were out and about. I'd learned to just smile and pretend I wasn't listening when people he'd treated at work would start discussing stuff with him right in front of me. Not that any of them ever seemed to care about the privacy of their health problems; some even tried to get me to join in which I always found amusing.

The waitress arrived, giving me a smile before turning to Simon. Her face fell momentarily while Simon quickly looked down at the table, then she turned back to me with a overly bright smile.

Interesting.

"What can I get y'all to drink?"

"I'll just have a water please."

"Same," Simon said, only looking up when the girl took off.

"What the hell?"

He reached across the table and covered my hand with his, face red. "She uh...she was one of the women I went on a date with that never called me back."

"Awkward," I sang, repeating his words of just a few minute ago, bringing a grin to his lips. "Did you know she worked here?"

"No." He shook his head. "It was a while ago, but she said she worked at the theater then. I come here rather often though, so she must have just started."

She came back then, gently placing the water on the table before pulling out her pad again. "Are you ready to order?"

The question directed at me, I had to suppress a grin at the silliness of her behavior.

I ordered and when she looked at Simon, he smiled at her while still holding my hand.

"Good to see you, Lex."

She bit her lip, probably contemplating how nice she should be. "I'm fine, thanks for asking. What would you like?"

With that, I giggled and her face flushed. Simon ordered, then she stalked away.

"I'm so embarrassed right now."

"Why?" I took a sip of water and watched his eyes darken as I licked my lips. "She's the one who should be embarrassed. It was one date and she didn't call back, big deal. No reason to be rude."

At that, he chuckled. "I like how she said 'I'm fine, thanks for asking' even though I hadn't."

"Do you know what her deal is?"

"Ah..." he coughed. "I might. I don't, however, think it's appropriate to share."

I shrugged, realizing that he'd probably rejected her advances or something similar, and took another drink of my water. "I understand."

When our food arrived ten minutes later, a new waitress had replaced Lex, who explained she'd gotten sick and had to leave.

To which Simon and I, after the waitress left, busted out laughing at before enjoying our meal.

~*~

After lunch, another walk around town, a visit to the library and one food shopping trip later, we arrived back at his place.

Sitting on the couch as the room around us slowly darkened, Simon asked if I would spend the night.

"Are you sure? I wouldn't want to tempt you too badly..."

He pulled me onto his lap, positioning me so I was straddling him. "I was thinking," he whispered, his voice low and rumbling. "That I could - well, that you could lie in my bed naked and let me touch you."

I sucked in a breath as both his palms slid up and down my arms, his words giving me goosebumps. "Do I get to touch you too?"

He shook his head, automatically making me pout.

Snickering, he tapped my mouth. "You're gonna trip on that."

I stuck it out a bit further and in a flash, he held my head in place as he softly caught my lower lip between his teeth.

Then, our mouths were battling as I hung on for dear life. In one smooth motion, he held me while standing up and headed toward the stairs. Ending the kiss so he could get us to his room safely, I nibbled on his ear, causing him to moan and my stomach to clench with desire.

Quickly divesting me of my clothing, I bit my lip nervously as he checked me out from head to toe. When he reached out to touch me, I held up a hand.

"You gotta be naked too. Otherwise it would be weird."

I thought it'd be too much like I was his patient, and by the gleam in his eye, I figured he realized that as well.

He took off his shirt and unbuckled his belt, pulling it out and tossing it aside as I sat on the bed. As he reached for the button on his pants, he paused, glancing at me. "Do I have to be completely naked?"

I tipped my head to the side, smirking at his question. "Why wouldn't you be?"

He gulped. "If I keep my boxers on...any attempt to take them off would make me pause and stop. I'm not sure I can guarantee..."

My nipples tightened at the mental images flying through my brain as he stopped talking. Incapable of speaking at this point, I waved a hand and he took off his pants, only to promptly come over and plop me in the middle of the bed.

His 'don't move' had me giggling.

Now he straddled me as I lie staring up at him. "Let me know if you want to stop, okay?"

"I will," I promised, holding still even though the very nearness of him made me want to wiggle.

I closed my eyes, only to open one a minute later when he'd done nothing. "What are you doing?"

"Admiring you," he whispered. "Your body is so beautiful. I'm not sure what to do first."

Now I blushed. "Touch me."

He lifted a hand, only to lower it again.

With a snicker at his hesitance, I snagged his hand in mine and brought it to my breast. Surging up into his palm, I squeezed lightly, hinting that he should do the same thing. He did and I let go, his free hand coming up to give the same attention to my other breast as I closed my eyes again.

"They fit perfectly in my palms," he observed, the desire in his voice so thick my nipples pebbled tighter, eliciting a low moan from me.

I didn't know if he noticed or not, a question that was answered when his mouth closed around one, sucking and licking with an untutored enthusiasm I found endearing. He switched to the other one for a moment, then stopped. His right hand trailed down my stomach, stopping just above the center of me. When he didn't move again, I opened my eyes only to find him staring at me.

"May I?"

I didn't wonder why he asked me for permission. He knew my past, he had my agreement when I'd taken off all my clothes, but the gesture meant the world to me. He wanted to make sure I said okay, that I was ready for his touch.

And in that moment, I knew one thing for certain - I'd completely fallen in love with Simon.

"Yes, please," I begged, unsure if the truth could be heard in my voice.

He must have seen something in my face though, because in that moment, a breathtaking smile lit up his face. He leaned in toward me, covering my mouth and kissed me with a reverence that had my nose tingling, tears bubbling to the surface. Without breaking the contact of our lips, he changed positions, lying down beside me on his side.

His hand skimmed lower, lightly parting me, both of us gasping. I bent a leg to make it easier as two of his fingers slid up and down. I moaned into his mouth, unable to stop myself from pleading for more with a tiny thrust of my hips. Taking my cue, he slipped a digit in, followed by another within seconds.

"Elle." My name was a breath against my lips, the slow in and out of his fingers a torture, his thumb pleasuring me on the outside. "You should see you right now. I've never seen anything so delightful in my life. Your face is flushed, your eyes dreamy. I would do this every day just to see you this way, just for you."

I didn't know if it was his words, or the look in his eyes, or just the right amount of touching. Yet as he bent his head to take a nipple between his lips, the heat of his mouth and the barest scrape of teeth finished the job, sending me over the edge. I stiffened as the pleasure coursed through my veins and his head came up just as I shut my eyes, throwing my head back as I cried out.

"Wow," he exclaimed hungrily.

A bark of laughter escaped me as I lifted my eyelids, his deep green eyes focused on my face. He removed his fingers slowly, leaning over to kiss me.

"I...you're..." he closed his own eyes, swallowing rapidly before gazing at me again. "You're lovely."

I didn't know what to say, the enormity of my feelings engulfing me even though I didn't know how to voice them.

I think he knew that though. Within seconds, he had our bodies covered up and me enveloped in his arms.

"Night Elle," he uttered in my ear.

His soft words were the last thing I remembered before sleep claimed me.

# CHAPTER TWENTY

Sunday dawned bright and sunny, dashing my hopes of the party being rained out and therefore, saving me from having to go there.

I knew that technically, I didn't have to go. But, even Penny said Lyndsey was so excited to meet me that I couldn't justify missing her party all because the very idea filled me with anxiety.

Having spent the past preceding days cleaning and sorting the house, I packed a bunch of boxes into the back of the car. They were full of Liliana's stuff that I didn't want but was sure her children would want, Yvette especially, since I knew her to be the most sentimental of the bunch.

My phone buzzed as I got into the car.

A text from Simon: *'running late due to work, may be half hour or so late, sorry'* had me frowning. I hadn't planned on going into the party without him; however, I'd promised Penny I'd be there at exactly five-thirty to help out. Never one to break my promises, I'd just have to suck it up and not let my worry get the better of me.

Arriving two minutes early, I walked slowly up the driveway filled with cars, gathering that this would be mostly family and maybe a few friends from Lyndsey's daycare. Squeals of laughter filled the air as I reached the gate and walked through. Penny spotted me first, rushing over to hug me, only to glance behind me with a frown.

"Where is Simon?"

"He fell behind, he'll be here soon," I assured her with a smile. "Um, wasn't I supposed to be helping you prepare?"

She laughed. "Yep, but I was up early so I just did it myself. Good thing too, people arrived an hour early!"

Most of the guests, from the looks of it. But where was Stefan?

Before I could respond, or locate the person I wanted to avoid the most, Lyndsey broke away from the group of kids, running toward me with a grin.

"Auntie Liz!" She wrapped her arms around my waist and looked up at me. "You came to my party!"

"Of course I did. I wouldn't miss it for the world." Even if I had considered bailing.

I picked her up, propping her on one hip as I walked her back to her friends.

She chattered in my ear in the way only an almost four year old could. After a few minutes, she kissed me on the cheek and asked to be let down. She ran off after another kid as I caught sight of Yvette.

"Hey Yvette," I said in a soft voice as I approached her.

For once, she didn't glare, although she seemed rather glum to me.

"Hi," she mumbled. "Some party huh?"

I shrugged. "It's for a bunch of preschoolers," I replied with a laugh. "However, there are some boxes of your moms stuff from the house in my trunk, if you want to go through them first."

She smiled, which I accepted as my thanks considering she took off an instant later.

When I saw Stefan break away from a group across the yard and walk toward me, I panicked. I had invited Simon so I wouldn't have any chance of being cornered by Stefan. I wasn't ready to talk and I wasn't sure I ever would be. The sudden urge to get sick had me spinning on my heel and running inside the house. I made it to the bathroom before getting ill, only to have the door open behind me seconds later.

"I'm in here!"

"Fucks sake, Ellie," Stefan growled, crouching next to me and holding my hair out of the way. "Let me help."

I moaned, my stomach heaving. I didn't want him here. Embarrassed at my reaction, it turned into anger with him for being so damn nice when all I wanted to do was yell at him, along with irritation at Simon for not being here even though I knew he couldn't help it. I should've waited but I stupidly thought I could deal with this on my own for a little bit.

I swatted his hand away, scrambling up and over to the sink to wash my mouth out. Stefan held his hand out, which I promptly pushed away from me.

"Knock it off! Take this." He snatched my hand in his and shoved something into it.

Looking down, I saw a white and red peppermint. Well, now I knew how he always had fresh breath.

Popping it in my mouth, I instantly moved it around with my tongue to coat my mouth with the taste. Stefan just stood there, watching me, not saying a word. His hands gripped the counter, an observation made only because I refused to look him in the face. I didn't have to because I knew what I'd see. Want. Hunger. Maybe even need.

I didn't need him. I thought I had, especially when I'd first seen him again.

I'd been wrong when comparing the passion of the two men. Stefan and I's fervor was fire too. However, unlike with Simon, it was overwhelming - an inferno that swept through without a thought for the destruction it brought. He hadn't meant to hurt me, but he had all the same. It didn't matter that he'd only left because I pushed him away, not to me. I couldn't see past what he'd done. I couldn't say if it would have changed anything had it happened a year or two later; the fact it had been within months had blown out the answering flame in me.

In the end, he deserved my honesty. I wouldn't keep his hope alive, knowing it would be cruel. And I wasn't a vicious person, for all the hurt I'd caused years ago. I'd been hurting badly and in the face of my rejection, so had he. But we couldn't go backward, it just wasn't possible. And starting over was an illusion - we couldn't pretend things hadn't happened. Even people who 'moved past' their hurts still carried them inside; the reminder of his hurt just happened to be another living, breathing human being he'd had with someone who'd pretended to be my friend the whole time.

I could forgive him for keeping it from me, for the way he'd revealed his secret and it was only fair that I did. We'd both messed up. Yet, that didn't mean we had a future.

I knew I'd never get over it. Even if it were completely selfish of me, at least I could admit my faults. As I tried to summon up the courage to tell him we were over forever, he spoke first.

"He can't love you like I can."

"Of course not," I countered, still focused on his hands. "Nobody can love me like you can. The good thing is, there is not just one way to love somebody."

"Damn it, Ellie! Look at me," he commanded.

I almost didn't, yet I heard it. The crack in his voice, the slight desperation, as if he knew what words were coming next and hoped to convince me not to voice them.

I dragged my eyes to his, watching as he saw all he needed to see in my face.

"Why?" The word came out so low, I would have missed it had I not been looking at him. "Why won't you forgive me? I didn't know, I didn't. She knew all along where you were, knew I searched for you and yet, pretended she had no—"

"Stop," I cut him off, his words just angering me. "She has nothing to do with *you* not telling me the truth before you took me with you to the hospital. You had plenty of time."

I straightened up, everything I wanted to say blurting out of me as I stabbed him in the chest with one finger.

"What did you think? That you could just fuck your way back into my life, hoping that when you finally told me I'd just roll over and take it? Love or no love, you lied to me. Whether that was by omission or a blatant act of deception makes no difference!"

He opened his mouth to speak but I gave him no opportunity.

"I do forgive you. I was hurt, I hurt you and in return, you did what you did. That's it though. It's over, Stefan. You can stop waiting because there is nothing to wait for."

His face paled as what I had just told him sunk in. "Ellie, please..."

I shook my head, my hand dropping to my side.

"When you were at my place, right before we slept together again for the first time, I questioned whether you were the Stefan I'd always known. You couldn't possibly have stayed the same, I thought. You had to have changed." I didn't take my eyes away from his. I wanted him to get what I had to say so there were no misunderstandings. "Thing is, you didn't. You're older and you take care of yourself better, but that's it. Not me. I changed that night. I wanted to have hope so badly when you walked back into my life; truth is, there never was any."

He took a shuddering breath, shaking his head even as his face paled even further. "That's not true—"

"Don't." I put up a hand, a sad smile on my face. "I loved you, I truly did. Had things happened differently, had I not been..." I couldn't even say the words. Clearing my throat, I continued, "If things were different, I think we would have been fine. But it happened, and my whole life...it became something else. I still love you now, but it's the kind of love you have for someone you used to know and be close to. I don't love you like you love me, and I never will."

He opened his mouth as if to say something.

"Elle."

I whirled around at the sound of Simon's voice.

Not saying anything else, he held out his hand.

I wondered how much he'd heard, thought I didn't dare glance back at Stefan.

Instead, I stepped forward and placed my hand in his.

As we walked away, I heard Stefan curse and slam the door shut.

~*~

A few moments after we stepped outside, the time had arrived for cake and ice cream, leaving us all standing so close to the table that speaking to Simon wasn't possible. Much as I'm sure he had something to say about what he'd no doubt heard, I was glad it wouldn't be until later.

Just when Evan started to head in and find Stefan, he walked outside. He didn't look at me, his eyes averted as he placed one hand on his daughters shoulder and started off the singing.

Lyndsey clapped giddily as everybody sang, only to puff over and over to blow out the candles, which re-lit automatically. The adults laughed for a few moments, with Stefan to leaning over with a laugh to blow them out a final time.

Before long the sky clouded and everyone rushed to finish up, thanking Penny for the lovely party and collecting their children to leave.

Penny asked me to help her get stuff inside to which I readily agreed. On another trip outside to collect stuff, I noticed Lyndsey leaving with one of her friends. Stefan and Grace stood near the table, their body language indicating that they were having an intense argument. I searched around for Simon, only to see him standing near the gate talking to Evan. Yvette, Adrian and Jerome sat at another table, and Yvette stood up as I approached.

In what seemed like the slowest few seconds of my life, the undercurrent I hadn't known to be there erupted as she reached my side.

"You had no right to invite *him* to the party," Yvette hissed at me. "It was for family and Lyndsey's friends only."

Not in the mood for this after my encounter with Stefan or to try and figure out why her attitude had reappeared, I glared at her.

"Oh, so *now* you wanna refer to me as family? That's rich!"

She shoved me and I stumbled, falling to the ground. Stefan ran over to grab Yvette's arm, as Simon appeared out of nowhere to help me up. Everyone else came running as I stood up, with Grace standing to the side, wide eyed.

"What the fuck is your problem, Yvette?" I yelled now, fed up.

She didn't say anything, just burst into sobs, which had four of her siblings glaring at me.

"What did you say to her?" That came from Stefan and with his automatic assumption that I'd said something to make her push me, I lost my temper completely.

"Oh, right, so she's being a total bitch to me and I'm automatically who you fucking blame? She approached me, not the other way around! She pushed me!"

I saw Penny rushing toward us from the corner of my eye as the rest of them looked away from me to Yvette.

"She told me I had no right to invite Simon to this party; that it was for family only," I persisted. "All I said was that it was rich of her to refer to me as family. She's made it clear before that I am not!"

"W-why are you even here?" Yvette wailed, breaking free of Stefan's hold. "You don't even belong here!"

"All right, what in the world is going on?" Penny arrived and Yvette ignored her, her body shaking with rage that confused me.

"You don't care about us, you only care about yourself," Yvette spat out, wiping the tears away from her eyes in a fury. "You hurt my brother, not only once but twice and think you can just waltz in here—"

"Oh, I hurt him twice? In case you didn't hear, he lied to me! Not to mention, which one of you had the balls to tell me the truth, huh?" I pointed at Grace, who looked ready to flee at any moment. "You! Certainly not you, right? How long were you after him, huh Grace? When I left, did you dance with glee at having the chance to get Stefan? Didn't work out for ya, did it though? You fucked him and deliberately got knocked up but it didn't work, did it? Then, you lie to him and me for years, are you proud of—"

"ENOUGH!"

All eyes flew to Simon, his face thunderous, as he cut off my rant. I sucked in a breath, having never heard him raise his voice before and instantly looked down at the ground.

"Penny invited me," he informed Yvette with a pointed look. "I would have been here either way, but your behavior is appalling. Violence is *not* the answer—" she opened her mouth but he continued in a louder tone. "*And* you are not a child so I'd advise you quit acting like one."

"That's right, I did invite him," Penny agreed, giving Yvette a dirty look. "You owe Elizabeth an apology."

I brought my head up at this. I didn't understand for a moment, until I realized that Simon had already been invited by the time he'd had me ask him. My invitation had been a declaration for him from me that he was what I wanted and nothing else.

"I don't owe that selfish bitch anything!" Yvette snapped in reply as she stomped off.

That didn't end the conversation though.

"As for you two," Simon said with a frown at Grace and Stefan. "Both of you were in the wrong."

They both started to speak but he held up a hand.

"I don't care. I'm not a doctor right now, I'm the man dating Elle standing in the middle of this damned mess. This whole thing is, quite frankly, disgusting. You should both be ashamed at your absolute lack of fucking common sense in dealing with the situation."

Stefan's mouth dropped open, Grace started crying, and Simon looked over at me.

"And you," he said, his voice dripping with his disappointment in me. "I expected better from you. Such a display in retaliation doesn't flatter you."

With that, he turned on his heel and my eyes filled with tears.

Seconds later, the sky opened up, rain pouring down with perfect timing to join me in my embarrassment.

# CHAPTER TWENTY-ONE

Three days passed without a word from Simon.

No calls, no texts. No response to my many messages. He'd declared to everyone at the party that we were dating but it sure didn't feel that way now.

I knew this was him ignoring me. He'd always call me, even if it would only last five minutes until he needed to get some sleep.

I also knew that I deserved it.

There wasn't an excuse for my behavior. Even though Yvette had pushed me, I shouldn't have responded that way. Commenting had only made things worse, not better. Walking away would have been smarter.

Worse than my retaliation at Yvette, was the indisputable fact I'd been wrong to be so rude to Grace. In the moment, it had felt good but in truth, it had been a cruel thing to do. I snapped because up until then, she'd said nothing to me since the moment I found out she'd had a baby with my ex-boyfriend. She wouldn't look at me, had ignored me the few times I'd run into her and, most of all, she hadn't even bothered to say sorry for lying to me all these years.

It would be hard to apologize to someone who didn't seem to feel sorry for any of her actions. Yet, I knew I would have to.

But first, I needed to get Simon to talk to me. I missed him. I hadn't even told him I loved him.

He probably thought of my little display as proof that I wanted Stefan.

Wrong, so wrong. *He* was the man I dreamed of now.

Before I thought it through clearly, I left the house. Deciding to walk since it was nice out, I quickly came to regret not driving.

Far enough from home yet close enough to Simon's place that turning around would take longer, the weather took a dive and rain cascaded down with no sign of letting up as rapidly as it had arrived.

Drenched to the bone, I cried as I kept walking.

Then, a horn honked. I looked over to find Grace driving slowly. The window lowered and she stopped the car, leaning over. "Get in!"

Still a good ten minutes away, I considered it for a brief second before shaking my head. I was almost there. I could do it without her help.

"Right now, Elizabeth," she shouted. "Or so help me, I'll hop out of this car and kick your ass."

I stood there, wondering if she'd actually do it, until she put the car in park and reached down to take off her seat belt. Not wishing to land us both in jail, I sloshed over to the car and got in.

"Haven't you heard of an umbrella?"

"Yes, but have you learned what birth control is?" I retorted, watching her face flame.

Instantly, I regretted it. Hadn't my mouth gotten me in enough trouble? "I'm sorry—"

"No! *I'm* sorry, Elizabeth," she said as she looked me straight in the eyes, her eyes shiny with unshed tears. "I...I never meant to lie. The whole thing was just a huge mistake. I wanted to tell you when it happened, b-but I froze up. I couldn't get the words out. As time passed, it got harder and harder until I just couldn't see the point anymore."

I wanted to yell at her, yet I couldn't. I knew what it was like to want to tell someone something, only to feel as if your whole world would fall apart if you did. To freeze up to the point you had to get away or you feared suffocating. Her secret had been nothing similar to mine, but it was her secret, not mine. I couldn't presume to know what it had felt like, because our situations weren't comparable.

"We never expected you to come home."

Her words pierced my heart, the truth in them unmistakable. Until Stefan had come careening back into my life, I hadn't even considered coming back home. If anything, I'd wanted to get even further away.

"Doctor Worthington was right. I should've told you, even if we thought you weren't coming back. Both Stefan and I handled it badly. You deserved to know the truth."

Even though she had finally apologized, her words didn't make me feel righteous.

They made me feel heartless. Cruel. Perhaps even vicious.

Stefan. My mother. Grace.

All of them. I should have told all of them.

People I loved and people who had loved me, all left out in the cold as to the change in my behavior.

As to why I'd left and had never bothered to call them, or come to visit.

I didn't know the right thing to say, searching for the words to tell her I understood. Yet she must have taken my silence as a refusal to speak of what had happened.

She looked away, her voice quavering as she put the car in gear and drove away from the curb. "Where were you going? I will take you there."

"Simon's."

I gave her an address and within minutes, she pulled in the driveway.

"You sure he's here?"

"No." I shrugged. "He won't answer my calls or texts."

"Do you want me to wait? It's still pouring…"

Shaking my head, I grabbed the door handle.

"T-thanks," she rushed ahead, no doubt afraid I'd get out before she finished. "For coming to the party, I mean. No matter what I did, I'm glad you realize its not her fault. She loves you."

I nodded, unable to speak for the tears clogging my throat and got out. She sat there, probably waiting for me to go to the door, but I didn't move. Finally she reversed and drove off.

I walked up to the door and stood as close as possible to avoid getting further drenched. I rang the doorbell. I knocked. Only silence greeted me.

Stupid. I was stupid for coming here without knowing if he was here or not. I probably should have looked in the garage window, but I wouldn't do it now with it still pouring just inches away from where I stood.

In one final, desperate attempt to get him to answer me, I sent him a text.

*'Are you home, I'm outside, raining. Need to talk. Please answer me.'*

A minute or two passed with no response. I couldn't be sure because my phone beeped at me and died. Even if he answered me, I'd have no way to know.

Cursing myself and the impulsive decision to come see a man who had obviously washed his hands of me, I curled into a ball near the corner of the door, hugging my knees and sobbing as I tried to figure out a way I could get home. I should have had Grace wait.

Shoulda, coulda, woulda.

More like idiot, idiot, idiot.

Just when I thought I'd have to walk home, the door moved behind me.

With a cry of surprise, I fell backward, sprawled on my back in his entryway. A very angry looking Simon stared down at me as he threw his hands in the air.

"What the *hell* do you think you are doing?"

~*~

I stared up at him, so glad to see him the ability to speak evaded me.

"What the—-? Where the hell is your car, Elle?"

He crouched down and gathered me into his arms. I wrapped mine around his neck while simultaneously placing my head in the crook of it. Shivering, an involuntary sob escaped, as the coldness finally registered.

"I've got you," he murmured. "What possessed you to walk here in the rain?"

"W-w-was s-sunny." Damn, my teeth chattering made talking painful. I refrained from attempting to explain any further, trying to warm my face using the heat of his throat. He was warm, I snuggled in closer and his arms tightened.

The door slammed shut and he strode away, carrying me up the stairs.

When he stopped walking I lifted my head, spotting his bed a few feet away.

"Can you stand? You gotta take these clothes off."

I nodded and he slowly lowered me. When I was steady, he quickly stripped me, the shivers wracking my body with every new rush of air against my skin. Walking away for a few seconds, he came back with a towel in hand. With the attitude of a man on a mission, he toweled me dry before guiding me over to the bed and under the blankets. I pulled them up over my head, curling into a ball to try and get warm. I didn't know what he was doing. I heard him moving around the room, opening and shutting drawers.

The next thing I knew, he crawled into bed and lay next to me. His arms wrapped around me from behind, his naked body flush against mine. He threw a leg over mine to hold them still, then the room fell silent. One of his hands rubbed my side, around to my stomach, down my leg slightly only to curve over my ass and back up my side. My trembling lessened, my teeth slowly chattering less and less until I sufficiently warmed up.

Still, he didn't speak. I wondered if he fell asleep, or if he wanted to warm me up only to take me back home once it was done. I felt him breathing against my neck, the weight of his arms and legs a delicious heaviness, and I sighed.

"Are you awake?"

My words were low, intentional in case he had fallen asleep. I didn't want to wake him. I needn't have worried.

"No."

I worried my lower lip with my teeth, unsure what to say. The silence deafening in its stillness, I tried to get him to talk me.

"Don't you have anything to say to me? Or yell at me?"

"No." A pause, a tightening of his arms around me sent my heart soaring. "Do you want me to yell at you?"

"I...I might deserve it."

When he placed a sweet kiss on my shoulder, I almost burst into tears.

"Don't be silly, Elle. I'd never yell at you."

"A-aren't you angry at me?" My voice trembled. I hated the way I felt, my vulnerability shining through. "You were ignoring me."

"No, not angry. Disappointed. Especially after what you'd said to Stefan, because I thought you were sincere."

I slammed my eyes shut, my estimation of what he'd thought of my words to Grace true. "I did mean it. But Grace hurt me and she hadn't even apologized. I—it was childish," I finished lamely.

"You ripped into her as if you were a jealous lover, Elle. Childish isn't the word."

"It's not what you think."

At that he flipped me onto my back before hovering over me, his eyes glinting devilishly. The very sight of it had me catching my breath.

"What is it then, Elle? Simon says you have to tell me."

His joke didn't have the desired effect, tears clouding my vision as I admitted the real reason I'd ripped into Grace like I had.

"She might've been mine," I whispered. "I'd have been a mother by now, maybe."

"I see," he said, his gaze thoughtful. "With Stefan?"

I frowned, nodding my head. "Back then, yes, it would have been." I sighed. "I'm hurt she lied to me, but I guess I am also jealous. I've always wanted to be a mother."

Simon gazed down at me, his whole body relaxing noticeably. "Is that all you want, Elle? A baby?"

"No," I shook my head, lowering my eyes to his lips as he unconsciously licked them. "I want more than that. I want a family."

"I know the feeling."

My mouth went dry at the sudden heat in his eyes.

"Flip onto your stomach," he said with a groan.

"Why?"

I swore his eyes burned brighter as he answered, smiling. "I want to touch you."

The very thought of him doing so made me want to moan. I turned over, unsure where to put my hands and finally just deciding I'd rest them on the pillow above my head. Simon nipped at my earlobe, chuckling in my ear.

"I may be a virgin in the literal sense of the word sweetie, but I know more than you think."

Oh, I knew that and counted on it. I wasn't going to admit it out loud though. For a moment, I thought he would say more, yet I found myself disappointed.

He skimmed his hands down, rubbing my shoulders, swirling his fingers, massaging my back with an occasional unexpected kiss to make me squirm. Then, they were on my ass; rubbing, assessing, appreciative. The low, rough timbre when he spoke gave me goosebumps.

"Some day - not tonight - I'm going to take you like this, with your lovely bottom lifted enough that I can slide home. All so I can watch you clutch those sheets in your hands, your body shuddering under mine in that beautiful submissive position."

I wished, right then, that I was the type of woman who could come from simply being spoken to. His voice would serve well for that.

Then, he moved. I couldn't see him. I felt him though as he slid up my body, his frame engulfing mine from above. His hands swallowed up mine, his mouth teasing my ear and neck as he licked and nibbled. I arched my ass up into him, my body on fire for something.

I wanted his touch on me, and I was sick of waiting.

"Are we going to have sex soon then?"

"Oh yes, tonight. Right now," he promised. "Except I want to see the face of the woman I love the first time. In case you're wondering, that would be you."

My breath hitched, the words slamming into me. "Simon…"

He gripped my hip with one hand, squeezing, comforting. "Elle."

216

I didn't hesitate. Isn't that what I came here to tell him? How much he meant to me.

He knew why I'd come.

No more hiding, no more lying to myself.

"Let me turn over."

He eased up and I turned back over, the recipient of a breathtaking smile I'd seen once before. Lifting a hand, I cupped his face in my hand; his head tilted automatically, seeking more as his eyes fluttered closed. With a bit of pressure, I brought his face to mine and kissed the corner of his mouth.

"I love you, too."

Like a storm unleashed, he took possession of my mouth as I wrapped my legs around him. He held my neck, his tongue diving into my mouth and around, moaning as he rocked into me. My hands slid around to grab his hair, battling with him for domination only to let him lead anyway.

His free hand roamed, down to my breast to cup it. A pinch of the nipple had him chuckling as I gasped. Our mouths broke apart. He leaned over and took the other nipple in his mouth, licking, sucking and nipping it as he tortured the other one by plucking it as if it were a string instrument. Then, he released my neck only to glide that hand toward the part that ached most for his touch.

The silky slide of his hand on a place where only inches away lie the part of him it prepared for excited me. I bucked against his hand and he chuckled against my skin as he skimmed down with two fingers, opening me with one, the other joining the first only moments later. Then started the torturous dance. Aching to get closer, to finally have him inside me had me pleading before long.

"Please Simon..."

"Open your eyes," he demanded.

I gave him what he wanted so he'd reciprocate in kind.

Bringing our bodies flush again, he held himself up with his arms once positioned just right.

Feeling him there, just out of reach, I mewled in protest.

Pressing a kiss to my lips, I felt his mouth curve as our gazes stayed connected.

"Simon says reach out and take what you want, Elle."

I relaxed one leg so I could reach down, the other clamped on to apply just enough pressure to force his body forward. I positioned him just right, surging upward at the same time I used my leg to grip him. Bringing the other up, I put my arms around his neck as I arched up again.

Simon's eyes closed on a groan, one hand going to hold my hip in what I gathered was a need for some control over movement. Still, he sunk inch by inch until finally, we couldn't get any closer and I wanted to sob with the joy of it. His eyes opened again, the green darkened with desire.

"I'm afraid to move." I laughed and his eyes widened. "I felt that."

Grinning now, I rotated my hips gently.

"Shi—" I heard him grit his teeth. "Oh god, don't."

"If you think this is ecstasy, pull back and push back in."

I loved seeing the look on his face as he did what I said. He sucked in a breath as he made as if to withdraw, only to let it out on a hiss once returned.

He stopped, gazing down at me.

"I don't think—" He gulped. "I should stop."

I shook my head, laughter bubbling in my throat.

"Kiss me, Simon and keep kissing me while you go as fast as you can."

The widening of his eyes made me bust out laughing.

"What about you?" His theatrical whisper even as I saw the strain of him keeping still made my heart flutter.

"Next round."

With one long stare at me, he did as I suggested. As our mouths made love to each other, ours bodies did the same. At first he hesitated, but then he gripped my ass with my guidance, taking a hint. In, out, speeding up until I thought he'd split me into a million pieces.

"Elle," he grunted, the word a praise on his lips as he gripped me tightly, with one last long moan into my mouth.

"Welcome to sex, Simon," I said with a giggle.

He rolled off, cracking open one eye.

"It's official, I've got two decades to make up for." He smiled. "Give me a few and we can get started on that."

Laughing, I playfully smacked him in the head with a pillow.

# CHAPTER TWENTY-TWO

"Why didn't you tell me?"

My mother looked up at me from underneath her wide brimmed straw hat, hands covered in soil from her garden. "It wasn't my place."

She focused on her task again.

"Penny pretty much said the same thing."

"Well honey, I honestly thought he'd tell you himself. When I realized he hadn't yet, I tried to warn you something was coming at least." Yes, she had, which was more than I could say for anybody else. "You still seeing that doctor?"

I almost asked how she knew, but then realized that while people didn't seem keen to share information with me, nobody minded sharing mine with everybody else.

"Yeah. His name is Simon." Something in my voice must have given away my feelings because she looked up at me again.

"Right, Simon. I've met him a few times." She smiled. "Is he it then? What about Stefan?"

She put her hand up after clapping them together to get the soil off and I helped her stand. We headed inside. As she poured us some drinks, I answered her question.

"I told him it was never going to happen."

"When was this?" She raised one eyebrow, taking a sip of her lemonade.

"Five days ago, at the party. You didn't come, were you even invited?"

She nodded. "Penny asked me to the original one, but when they moved it, I already had plans."

"Ah, well. There was a nice blow up at the end which started with Yvette yelling at me before pushing me to the ground."

"She did what?" My mother's voice rose in disbelief. "Why would she do such a thing? She's always so quiet!"

"Because Simon came there. I thought he came because I asked him to, but Penny actually invited him. Yvette said neither of us belonged there. That I wasn't family. Didn't shock me really, she hadn't liked me for a very long time. You remember her antics at the funeral, right?"

"Yeah, I do. Ever wonder why she dislikes you so much?"

"Yes. I wish I knew." I laughed. "She accused me of hurting her brother not once, but *twice*. I agree with blaming me for years ago, but now? As if him lying to me should have been something I just accepted."

"Sounds like she's trying to convince a certain somebody that he's better off without you."

Something in her statement had my eyebrows rising, as if she were saying...

No, she couldn't be.

Yvette had been around for so long that I forgot most of the time that she'd first been fostered by Liliana, then adopted at the age of twelve. She'd been an angry and depressed preteen, coming from a past involving an abusive alcoholic father and a drug addicted mother. Found roaming the streets at age ten, she had claimed her father had abandoned them and in desperation for drugs, her mother sold Yvette to a strange man. Who it was and how she'd ended up near to town had never been answered; she also hadn't cared to share.

Stefan had been eighteen when Yvette had come to live with them, twenty when he'd legally became her brother.

I threw my mother a disgusted face.

"They've been brother and sister since the moment she came to live with them, even if it took two years for it to be legal."

My mother shrugged. "It wouldn't be that weird. She knows he's not her brother. Just because he thinks of her as his sister doesn't mean she sees him that way."

I covered my face with my hands, groaning. "What makes you say this? I just...ugh."

"Her actions scream jealousy to me. You and Stefan were only friends when she first met you. Then, two years later, you and he were dating. She wasn't always mean to you. Didn't you ever wonder why the sudden change in her attitude?"

No, she certainly hadn't been. When he and I could drag her out of the house, she tagged along with such joy at being included. Even if we only went to the mall to walk around, she didn't care. Every time I left, for two straight years, she hugged me and told me she couldn't wait until we could do it again.

I rapidly began to feel sick.

Twelve years since Yvette had moved in, ten since she'd been adopted and Stefan and I had begun dating, and her attitude had done a one-eighty. I wouldn't have put it together like that then - even her family had simply assumed her to just 'being a teenager' and let it go. I had let it go too; I'd been aware of her past and never held it against her.

"Oh god, you're right!" I exclaimed with dawning horror. "I wonder if he knows."

"Don't you say a word to him," my mother retorted with a scowl. "No need to embarrass the poor girl. He most likely has no clue."

Just then, my phone lit up with a text message.

*'Can you come over? Wanna talk.'*

The message had come from Grace. After her kindness in picking me up the other day, and her apology, I realized I had yet to say sorry to her for my behavior at the party. I text her back.

*'Sure, at my moms, leaving soon.'*

I stood up and my mother did the same. "Okay, Grace wants to talk so I'm gonna go to her place."

"Tell her I said hi and that she should bring Lyndsey over so I can give her the gift I bought."

"Will do," I promised as she enveloped me in a hug.

Then I left, the remnants of the discussion I just had with my mom not far from my mind as I drove to Grace's house.

~*~

"Hello?" I opened Grace's front door, calling out as I stepped inside and shut the door. Not seeing her car outside, I wondered if the car was in the shop and entered the house. Nobody ever locked their doors here. Walking to the kitchen, I called out again. "Grace?"

Backtracking to the steps by the front door that headed upstairs, I took a step just as the door opened behind me.

I turned around to find Stefan standing there.

"What are you doing here?"

My eyebrows shot up. I put my hands on my hips and scowled. "Me? I was invited. What are *you* doing here?"

He grinned, closing the door. "I got a text from her asking me if I wanted Lyndsey for the afternoon."

"Isn't Lyndsey in daycare?"

"She's supposed to be." He shrugged. "I thought perhaps she'd not gone today."

"Well," I said with a sweep of my hand, realizing she had tricked both of us. "She's not here and I think it's safe to assume she's not going to be here."

Chuckling, he crossed his arms over his chest, his wide stance blocking me on the step so I only had one way to go. "A set up then. I just might forgive her for lying to me at this rate."

"And here I was, willing to apologize for my behavior to her at the party, but perhaps I've changed my mind."

He lifted a hand to my face, cupping my face in his hands. "Don't be that way. She's just trying to help," he said softly. "She royally screwed up and she knows it."

"Too little, too late."

I didn't move, I barely breathed. Just the feel of his hand against my face had my heart racing.

It had always been like this. He'd touch me and I'd just want to melt, to let him hold me, touch me, make me forget everything.

His next words shocked me.

"I hate the way you made me feel at that party. The way you've made me feel ever since you found out. You've no idea the torture I've endured the last five years. I didn't know where you were - I only knew you were safe because your mother said so. I begged her, many times through the years to just tell me where you were, but she always denied me even as she apologized. That you'd come back when you were ready. You never planned to though, did you?"

All I could do was shake my head as I stared at him. The words came through his teeth, his restraint evident even though the gentleness of his hand hadn't changed. His expression tightened, his mouth flattening at my response.

"I knew that. The fact she gave me your number just showed me that she'd given up. She didn't even think I could bring you back. You were so far gone from all of us, never giving us any thought. You didn't care how we felt, you only cared about yourself."

I stiffened at that and slapped his hand away.

"Don't even," he bit out before I could speak. "You can be righteous all you want but what you did to us, even for all your reasons, was just as despicable as Grace and I not telling you about having a child together."

Not thinking about the consequences of my actions, I laughed dryly. "Oh, so I suppose everybody in your life is being one hundred percent truthful at this point? If they all know how much lies hurt, have they told you all the things *they* are hiding?"

He blinked, the response obviously not one he expected. "What are you talking about? This is about you and me."

"Is it?" My voice rose as my ire increased. "I hid one thing - one thing! - and suddenly I'm the bad guy? I admitted I hurt you and I've said sorry. It *was* cruel of me to just push you out, but at the time I was in so much pain that I wanted to die. It's not the same thing as fucking my best friend and having a child together, and not telling me about it before you start sucking up to me!"

"Sucking up to you?" He shoved a hand through his hair, holding it for a second before letting go with a laugh. "Are you fucking kidding me? I have been devoted to you since the moment we met, Ellie! We have been friends since I was twelve and you were ten; we told each other everything. Did you care about that when you shut me out? No! No, you didn't! You treated me like I meant nothing!"

The pain on his face spoke volumes.

"If you want to pretend I mean nothing to you, that's fine," he continued, his voice breaking. "But don't you *dare* tell me I haven't changed, because I have. Don't pretend to know why I did or didn't do something. All I wanted was for you to come back home and even if you being in my arms only lasted a few weeks, it was better than never again."

"You would see it that way," I whispered. "You hurt me more by doing it that way."

"I would have hurt you either way!" He roared, throwing his hands in the air in a gesture of helplessness. "I wanted you so badly I said fuck the consequences, because it's not like we were friends anymore. We were nothing and you made us that way!"

I flinched, wishing that for just a moment, I could go back and changed how I'd handled it all.

"You're right," I admitted, my throat clogging with tears I refused to shed as I stared down at my hands. "I'm so sorry."

"I don't want you to be sorry, dammit. I want you to fix it."

I knew the feeling. In one particularly intense therapy session near the beginning of my new life far away from home, I'd cried about how nothing I did seemed to ease the pain.

*"It takes time, Elizabeth. You can't just will the pain away. You can only do so much. Sometimes, our brains are ready to move on faster than our hearts are. You will never escape what's happened, you can only learn to deal with it."*

*"I just want to fix it!" I cried.*

*But she'd simply said the same thing again.*

And eventually, she'd been right. The pain was just a dull ache now.

"I can't," I told him quietly. "And you know it."

"You really meant it, didn't you?" I heard the defeat in his voice at the reference to our conversation at the party.

I looked up, placing a hand on his shoulder as his eyes bore into mine.

"When I saw you again, how much I wanted to be near you again is all I thought about. Before then, you were constantly in my dreams. I missed you, so much it hurt. And when you came back into my life, once I'd gotten over the fear, I thought maybe this was it. Maybe we could be what we were. Problem is, nothing can ever be how it used to be. We can't turn back time, we can't pretend it didn't happen; we can only learn how to deal with what we have now."

"I know we can't forget," he rasped. "I know that. I just want to start again."

And with that, I cradled his face in my hand before leaning forward and softly pecking his cheek.

"I don't. I love him, Stefan. And he loves me. He is a good man. I will not hurt him. I've learned from my mistakes too."

He nodded and wrapped his arms around me, pulling me against him tightly. "I'll always love you, Ellie. Always."

I wish I could say I said it back, one last time. Meant it as much as he did.

Or that I'd changed my mind at his words and given in.

That I'd told him we could work this out.

But I didn't.

He let me go and walked out before I could say anything at all.

I had no way of knowing that those words would be the last I'd ever spoken to me.

Or that those moments were the very last time I'd see him alive.

# CHAPTER TWENTY-THREE

It was eight p.m. on a Saturday night several weeks later.

Simon and I were laying in bed watching T.V. when my phone rang.

He reached over to the side table and looked at the screen.

"It's Grace."

I waved him to put it back. "She's probably just calling to ask why I didn't come to the get together. I'll call her later."

I never told Grace what had happened, figuring Stefan had probably done the honors anyway. When I made it clear that things were serious with Simon, she agreed not to do anything like that again.

We weren't friends again, but we weren't enemies. I planned to move forward with my life, determined to put it all behind me at the very least. Plus, with Lyndsey wanting to see me more, being civil was imperative.

Simon, when I told him how Grace had set us up, only seemed amused. I didn't need to make it clear that nothing had happened, but I did anyway. Because I wanted to be open and honest with him. I truly had learned from my mistakes, just as I'd told Stefan I had. I'd be honest even if it hurt so badly I couldn't breathe. I didn't want to destroy what I had a second time.

"You may want to answer it," he said as it rang again, putting it in my hand.

I sighed, annoyed. "Hello?"

A hysterical Grace answered me, but I couldn't understand anything she said.

An unexplainable dread filled me the longer she babbled. "Slow down, Grace. I can't understand you."

Her crying in my ear escalated to the point I held the phone slightly away. Simon looked at with me a quizzical expression.

"Who? What? Damn it, give the phone to someone who is coherent!"

I heard the phone shuffling hands, Grace wailing for 'someone else' and finally, Evan came onto the line. "Elizabeth?"

Something in the soft desperation of his voice alarmed me. "What is going on Evan? Who is hurt?"

"Stefan."

My heart dropped into my stomach as I sat up. "What happened? Is he okay?"

"I don't know. One minute he was sitting on the edge of a table, the next he was on the ground. The ambulance just left—" He cut off and I heard Grace shouting in the background. "I—I gotta go."

He hung up before I could ask anything else.

"Elle, let's go."

I looked up at Simon, who at some point in the last minute had gotten up and put clothes on. He took the phone out of my hands and handed me something to wear.

Within minutes we were out the door and headed to the hospital.

I couldn't speak. At that point, I felt as if I were barely breathing.

Simon clutched my hand the whole way.

Even though I knew that emergencies were something he dealt with at work, his calm in this moment unnerved me even as it countered my panic. Then again, he hadn't been the one who'd had a bond with Stefan, a relationship. He wouldn't feel the pain I felt in that moment, which probably would end up being a good thing. I cried with worry the whole way there, hoping it wasn't serious. We may not be together, but I still cared.

*He just collapsed? He's a thirty year old man, they don't just collapse.*

I rushed inside after we arrived, full on running to the door as I left Simon behind.

The whole family sat in the waiting room. Lyndsey sat in Grace's lap, Evan hugging them both as they cried. Yvette sat sobbing, Adrian trying to comfort her as Jerome sat next to him, his face pale and withdrawn. None of them looked at me for more than a moment, other than Penny who jumped up to envelope me in a tight hug. Simon's hand on my back as he came up behind me announced his arrival, Penny pulling back from me to look him in the face.

"He just hit the ground, Simon. They said his heart stopped. He's thirty, he's too young for his heart to just stop, isn't he?"

Simon grimaced.

"They are trying to resuscitate him now," she continued on through her tears, not waiting for an answer as she turned around. "Come sit down, all we can do is wait."

We didn't even get the chance.

The doctor - later, Simon would tell me that his name was Maximilian Hawkins - came through the doors, his face severe.

For me, he didn't even have to speak. I knew before he even opened his mouth.

"I'm sorry," he said with a shake of his head. "We did everything…"

Simon's arms came around me to hold me up as I felt my knees give out. Penny, still holding onto my arm, slid to the floor with a cry. I don't know what the others did, my vision so blurred with tears I couldn't even see straight.

"How could you?" Yvette howled from across the room. I looked over, wandering who she was talking to. "You two are disgusting!"

She was in Evan's face now. Simon let go of me with a whisper to hang in there, heading over to stop her from doing something stupid.

He grabbed her arm as she ranted.

"He saw you! He saw you kissing and how could you? That's his daughter's mother! You're sick!"

Evan didn't say anything, his head bowed.

"I love him and you killed him! You fucking killed him!"

At that his head came up, his eyes wide.

I watched as Simon whispered down to her, pulling her away even though she was reluctant.

"I don't care!" She shouted at whatever he said, her eyes shooting daggers at me as he went to take her outside. "I hate all of you! I love him and now I'll never get to tell him. I hate you!"

I stood there, feeling as helpless as the doctor who'd had to deliver the news.

Nothing would ever be the same for any of us.

Not for his daughter.

Not for his siblings.

Not for Grace.

Not for me.

And not for Yvette, whose love for Stefan would forever go unrequited. Even though I'd guessed the truth, my heart broke for her in that moment, because suddenly, everything she wanted had been torn from her.

So I did the only thing I could do in that moment.

I crouched down and wrapped Penny in my arms.

~*~

I felt punished.

Still lying in bed as Simon got up to get coffee, I didn't want to move.

The days had passed in a blur, I didn't even know what day it was or how many had passed.

I only knew today was the day of the funeral because Simon had told me.

Stefan had died of Hypertrophic cardiomyopathy.

Or, as Simon had explained to me and his family in basic terms, an enlarged heart.

Due to the fact it was such a shock, it was safe to assume that Stefan had felt fine. With no symptoms, he'd have never seen it coming, which means nobody else would have either. But it didn't take away the pain.

*Nobody had killed him.*

I kept repeating that over and over to myself but the truth is, I felt like I had.

Grace and Evan probably felt as if they had.

And Yvette, in her grief, blamed all of us.

As I heard Simon come back into the room, I didn't bother to look at him. I didn't really want to go. I hadn't even gone to the wake the night before because I hadn't been sure I could handle it. When Simon pulled the blankets off of me though, I knew it was time to face the world.

"Let's get you a shower Elle. I hate to tell you this, but you stink."

His voice was soft and sweet, yet the tears still welled in my eyes. His, filled with worry, didn't look away from me as he held out his hand.

"Come on, I'll do all the work. All you've gotta do is just stand there."

I took his hand and before long, we were in the shower. Wetting my hair, he had me turn around so he could wash it. His fingers massaged my scalp, my head tilting back as I moaned at the sheer loveliness of it. I hadn't let him touch me since that night at the hospital, afraid if anybody put their hands on me I would break down and cry.

His hands slid down to shampoo the rest of my hair, before gently turning me around and rinsing it out. I kept my eyes closed even after he was finished. Neither of us spoke as he started washing me with a loofah, foamy with the body wash I'd brought over to use here. Shoulders and down my arms, only to come back up under them; then my breasts, the nipples perking as the material glided over them and

I heard his sharp inhale. Then down the rest of my body and to my legs.

"Turn around."

I did, the front cleaned off by the water as he continued washing my backside. His strokes slowed down, lingered. I wanted him to touch me, especially as he slid it between my legs and thought he would until he spoke.

"Okay, all done. My turn."

I opened my eyes finally, pivoting to face him and rinsed off the rest of the soap, only to find him staring at me with an undeniable hunger on his face. His statement took on a whole different meaning and I smiled for the first time in what felt like forever.

"Are you talking about washing yourself or putting your hands all over me?" My voice came out low, raw with emotions I refused to let out.

He dropped the loofah and grabbed me around the waist, pulling me against him roughly.

"It's so good to hear you talk," he said into my ear. "I've been worried."

At first, I'd been worried too. The despondency I felt at hearing Stefan was dead had been near to what I'd felt all those years ago. The sorrow was different, but the ache...ah, the ache didn't care. My heart wept, even though I didn't dare cry. The tears would come, but not yet. First, I had to get through the day. And what I wanted right now, was something to get me through it.

"I need you, Simon." The words, said on a breath, had him pulling his head back, his eyes searching mine.

"Right now?"

"Please," I begged. "I don't want sweet. Make me forget, even for just a moment."

"Grab onto the bar," he ordered with a nod, turning to put my back against the side wall. "And hold on."

I didn't know why I needed the bar until he got down in front of me and glanced back to make sure I did as told. I grabbed it, my eyes widening as he placed my legs over his shoulders, holding my ass in his hands. No further words, just moans as his mouth was on me, teasing me, loving me. My grip on the bar so tight I thought I'd rip it straight off the wall, he shifted to support me with one hand, while the other moved around to join in with his lips.

One finger, then two, not sliding in and out but stroking me on the inside. A sob escaped but whether it was from what he was doing or the emotions trying to escape me in a moment when I wasn't actively trying to stomp them out, I never knew. Pleasure ripped through me and I shook with the power of it. Not even sure when Simon had slid back up as he lifted my legs up and around his frame, bracing my body with one hand as he guided himself to me with the other.

He slid in with ease, my body opening up for him, greedy. I kissed him, my hands releasing the bar and gripping his hair as I recognized how badly I'd needed this, desired *him*, to feel connected. His movements were otherwise slow and languorous, each slow slide out and back in a wonderful torture. I wiggled, trying to get closer, the intimacy of our entwined bodies not enough for me in that moment. For one insane second I wished that I could get inside him, share my pain with him in a way I never shared with anybody else.

So I told him with my mouth and body, clinging to him like a lifeline, our bodies as close as two people could be from head to where we joined. And when he finally stiffened and stilled, his fingers gripping my thighs firmly as he moaned, the tears that had wanted to escape from deep inside me finally did. I could no longer hold them inside so I held on to him instead.

Simon slid us both to the floor and as the water pounded on us from above, he held me in his arms without saying a word as I cried.

~\*~

I stood in between Simon and Penny during Stefan's burial. Yvette stood close to her dad at the opposite end and Richard clutched her closely. All the other siblings stood in one solid line, holding hands. Grace and Lyndsey sat in front of the line. The sound of Lyndsey's tears broke my heart the most.

So many other people had come that I found myself surprised. I hadn't known he'd meant so much to so many people, yet it should've been obvious to me that everybody loved Stefan. He'd been fun, lively, smart, kind and a good man through and through.

It also wasn't like his mother's funeral had been. The sun shined now, bright and without mercy. I felt as if I were going to melt.

I almost smiled at the thought, since one of Stefan's favorite things to do involved turning me into a puddle of want.

When it came time to leave, I walked up to the casket and put one hand gently upon it while placing a pink carnation with the other.

"I'll never forget you," I whispered, kissing the tips of my fingers and pressing them down on the wood reverently. "You'll always be my first love."

A hand around my arm had me looking up, expecting to find Simon only to see Penny, her eyes bright with unshed tears.

"He knew," she said quietly. "He wasn't angry; he even told me that he was truly happy for you. That it had been a very long time since he'd seen you with such happiness in your eyes. He didn't die angry with you. He said you had found your Conley, whatever that means." She tilted her head to the side, a soft curious smile on her face.

My eyes filled, her words comforting me and shocking me all at once. I hadn't realized he remembered his words to me about finding the perfect man, let alone that he'd mentioned it to someone else. "Thank you. It was a character in a story…" My voice choked and I shook my head.

She said no more, patting my arm. We stood there for a few more moments until others walked up. Penny tugged me away gently, escorting me back toward Simon. Reaching his side, she released my arm.

"We will all need to find peace and I knew that is something you'd need to know to find it. All he ever wanted was your happiness. We all do."

I hugged her, the words she spoke so true, even though I hadn't known I'd needed to hear them.

"Get some rest Penny."

"You too." She threw me one final smile and returned to her family.

"Let's go home," Simon suggested, grabbing my hand in his. "You need some rest yourself. You still look really tired."

"Okay." He wouldn't get any argument from me about that.

I leaned against him as we walked, closing my eyes as he lead the way. I didn't worry that I'd trip and fall, because even if I did, he'd be there to catch me. As a gentle breeze hit my face, I had the sudden urge to look back and I opened my eyes, looking over my shoulder.

Yvette sat on her knees next to the casket, her palms flat against the sides with her head bowed. Her shoulders shook as Richard stood over her, a helpless look on his face. Knowing she'd deny my comfort even if I went back to give it to her, I turned back around with the determination to do something, anything to ease her pain if at all possible.

And as an idea came to me, so did the first stirrings of peace.

It may not be enough, but I'd certainly do all I could for Yvette to give her some as well.

# CHAPTER TWENTY-FOUR

It took a few weeks but finally, my plan fell into place.

I walked into Penny's house, knowing she would be expecting me. Yvette wouldn't be though, which is where she'd been staying since she'd graduated college. I knew if I asked her to meet me that she never would.

Entering the living room, Yvette didn't see me at first. She sat in a chair facing away from the door while Penny lounged on the couch, both of them reading books. Penny had been shocked to discover Yvette's feelings for Stefan, telling me she'd made it perfectly clear to Yvette that it didn't make her any less of a sister. Really though, who didn't like Penny? She was a kind and considerate woman and not for the first time, I wondered who her boyfriend was.

"Uh, hey," I finally said after a few seconds. They were both so engrossed in their books that they jumped at the sound of my voice.

"What are *you* doing here?"

Of course Yvette was the first to speak. She slammed her book shut as Penny stood up.

"Elizabeth's here at my invitation, Yvette. She'd like to talk to you."

"And I want to talk to her because...?"

Penny rolled her eyes and walked toward me. Giving me a quick hug, she exited the room.

I walked over to the couch and sat down. Yvette didn't automatically get up so I took that as a good sign. Instead she continued to stare down at the book, her posture stiff.

I decided to just jump right in and hope she listened.

"You were right. I did hurt Stefan twice, not just once."

Her head snapped up, eyes full of surprise at my admission.

"However, he hurt me too. It's not up for debate," I held up a hand as she opened her mouth as if to say something. "The first time happened because I'd been hurt and so caught up in my own pain that I didn't see the pain I caused him. He walked away because I pushed him, when if he had known the truth, he wouldn't have. Then, I saw him again and part of me wanted so badly to be the person I used to be. To be happy and in love and with him, like I'd always wanted. He had a way of making me feel things nobody else ever had, but he could also piss me off too."

She ducked her head, but not before I noticed the tears in her eyes.

"Problem was, even when I'd come back here, I told him I wasn't sure we'd ever have another relationship. I had hope but I had so much more doubt about everything. I spent all the time away just trying to put myself back together. I didn't want to fall apart again. I promised him nothing in regards to being with me, only the opportunity to try. Unfortunately for him, he took too long in telling me something he should have told me from the very beginning. It may not have changed anything, but not telling me was the worst thing he could have done. It was dishonest and hurtful."

"He planned to tell you," she said without looking up. "He spent years talking about you, but he wasn't naive. He knew you would be hurt. He just thought…"

"I know what he thought; he told me." I took a deep breath, collecting my thoughts. "The last time I saw him, we had a nasty fight, but even at the end, he just hugged me and told me he loved me, that he would always love me. I didn't feel like I deserved it."

"Why are you telling me this?" She whispered, her anguish obvious.

"Because I saw your pain. And I realized that it's exactly how I made him feel and it made me feel absolutely terrible. I was all he ever wanted yet he couldn't have me in the end."

"It wasn't fair!" She wailed, her tear filled eyes meeting mine. "I loved him, no matter what! Even when he found out Grace was pregnant, I still loved him. I supported him and all I ever wanted was him. We didn't grow up together, we weren't *really* siblings yet he always treated me that way. Even when—"

She cut off, covering her mouth with one hand as if she'd been about to reveal too much, but it was too late. "He knew how you felt?"

"Yes." Her face flamed at the admission and she lifted her chin defiantly. "I...I tried to tell him how I felt once and I couldn't. So instead, I kissed him."

My mouth dropped open. "When?"

"Two years ago. We...we were all together at the house drinking. It was Christmas. That had been the first time he drank since right after you left and, well, you know. We'd gone to the kitchen to get more when we both tried to pass through the door and there it was, the mistletoe." Her face grew soft, the look on it so wistful I hurt for her. "He leaned down and kissed my cheek, whispering 'Merry Christmas, Yvette'. It was so sweet and I was sick of pretending I didn't feel anything so before he could back away, I put my arms around his neck and just put my lips to his. He—he was so stunned at first he just stood there. Then, he pushed me away gently and shook his head. 'No.' That's all he said. He walked away but he never treated me any differently. It was as if it never happened."

Wow. I sat back, crossing my arms over my chest. "Maybe he didn't bring it up because he didn't want to embarrass you," I offered.

"Yeah, maybe." She didn't sound convinced and I knew she'd always wonder why he didn't say anything. It didn't surprise me that he pretended it never happened though; he probably hadn't wanted to hurt her by having to make it very clear he didn't think of her that way.

"So," I cleared my throat. "I didn't only come here to talk to you. I came here to ask you something."

She didn't say anything, just lifted a brow as if to say 'what'.

I held papers out to her and she blinked, as if only just realizing I'd been carrying them. Taking them from me, she looked down at them for several minutes, silent.

When she lifted her head, her face was full of confusion. "This is a lease...to the house. To mom's house."

"Yes it is. It is mine now, and I could even sell it if I wanted too. But I won't. I believe Lyndsey should have the option to have the house when she grows up. However, you can lease it from me if you want. For free. I don't want or need your money; I've got plenty of my own that I saved."

She blinked as if she didn't believe I was offering her such a thing.

"I didn't understand why you were mean to me for so long. It wasn't right, but I understand now and I'm not mad. I can't give you Stefan, but I can give you this, since he told me the home would have been his anyway. You can stay as long as you want."

Her face crumpled, her shoulders shaking as she started sobbing, head in hands.

Penny came back into the room then. "What in the world?"

I swear that's Penny's favorite phrase and I smiled. "I think she's overwhelmed."

Yvette snorts. Concerned that she can't breathe or something, I started to reach over until I realized that she was laughing at my comment through her sobs. She stood up abruptly and for a second, I feared she would flee the room without answering me. Instead, she leaned over and pulled me into a hug, shocking the shit out of me.

"I accept. Thank you so, so much!"

Before I could do or say anything back, she released me and sat back down, wiping the tears from her face with a swipe of the back of her hand.

"You're welcome. You can move in in two weeks."

I planned to move in with Simon. I'd told him my plan and he seemed quite happy at the idea of me coming to live with him. I can admit I was pretty damn excited myself.

"Okay, so I just have to sign?"

I handed her a pen with a nod. She took it and quickly signed every place before handing one copy back to me.

With a smile, I stood up, sighing. "I hate to run, but Simon's planned dinner and I can't be late!"

"I...I'm really happy for you Elizabeth. Simon's a nice guy."

Yvette's kind words surprised me but I didn't let it show. I just grinned wider, feeling better than I had in a really long time. "Thanks, he is."

Penny walked me to the door. Opening it, she turned and gave me a hug.

"Tell Simon I said hi and that he better treat you right!"

I laughed, squeezing her back. "Will do."

Just then, the highly irritating smell of skunk reached us and as Penny wrinkled her nose, a strong wave of nausea had me getting sick in her bushes.

Penny cracked up. "That's a bit of a strong reaction to a common smell around here, Elizabeth. What are you, pregnant?"

I heard the humor in her voice, yet suddenly, I wasn't laughing.

I must have gone pale because Penny grabbed my arm as I straightened up. "Geez, Elizabeth, I was just kidding. You don't have to look so freaked out."

"Oh, shit!"

Her mouth dropped open as I wracked my brain.

How was this possible?

When was my last period? Crap, too many weeks ago! Did I miss my pill? When did I miss it? Then it dawned on me.

*Stefan's funeral.*

"Oh, fuck! Shit, shit, shit!" I ran a hand through my hair, trying to calm myself even as my chest tightened with anxiety.

"Okaaaaaaaay," Penny said with a laugh, dragging me back inside. "Good thing I keep a test 'just in case' I start to get freaked out myself. Let's go."

Once in her bathroom, she handed me the test and then closed the door, leaving me inside as I stared down at the test with a mixture of terror and hope.

Did I want a baby? With Simon?

Yes, yes I did.

Now I was afraid the test would say no and it would just turn out to be all the stress getting to me.

I did as the instructions said, then sat the test on the counter.

After a few moments, I picked it up to look at the results, and promptly burst into tears.

~*~

"Elle?"

I looked at Simon across the table, his brows furrowed in concern. "Are you all right?"

No, no I wasn't. I felt sick.

"I'm...um, I'm not really hungry right now."

"Is something wrong?"

"Ah, no." I shook my head and stood up. "I'm gonna go lay down, okay?"

I didn't wait for him to reply.

*Stupid.*

I scolded myself all the way up the steps and into the bathroom.

Through brushing my teeth. And changing for bed.

Then, lying in bed with the curtains closed and the light out.

I knew it wouldn't be long before he came in wanting to know what was wrong.

It didn't.

Soon, the bed tipped as he climbed in. Like every other night, he wrapped me in his arms, his left leg thrown over mine as he pulled me close to snuggle. This wasn't like every other night though. Tonight would be the night everything changed, if he wasn't ready for the things I was.

He didn't say anything. Just caressed me softly with one hand on my leg, my side, my stomach. Then, a trail of kisses that started off on the back of my neck and went down my shoulder. I'd been lying there rather stiff and slowly, I softened, his touch comforting.

The room was silent except for our breathing.

Yet it still had never seemed so loud.

"Elle? Talk to me." His voice was hushed, consoling. "I wanted to talk to you myself, but you left the table before I could."

My mouth went dry, my heart speeding up. "About what?"

"Turn over."

He moved enough to let me do so and thanks to the hallway light he'd left on, I could see him perfectly. He looked so relaxed and happy. He leaned in and kissed me, automatically seeking entrance. Too soon, he pulled back.

"There. You look less serious."

I smiled even as my nose tingled with tears I wasn't sure I could hold back much longer.

"You see," he said with a wink. "I brought you a present home. Do you want it?"

I nodded, not trusting myself to speak at this point.

He reached down and into his pocket, pulling out a box.

I sucked in a breath as he took my hand in his.

Oh god, was he going to propose?

He was!

*Wait! Wait!*

My mind screamed at me but all I could do was stare at him.

"I love you, Elle. I know this might be rather soon, but I'm a man who knows what he wants."

He opened the box and my eyes widened, the gorgeous diamond ring inside winking at me even in the weak light shining into the room. My heart pounded as he pulled it out and held it between two fingers.

Kissing my hand, he squeezed gently as he looked straight into my eyes. "Elle, will you make an honest man out of me and marry me?"

My heart felt as if it were going to pound right out of my chest. I felt happy and sick all at once.

So I did the only thing a girl in my situation could do. "Simon, I'm pregnant."

He froze, the grip on my hand tightening as I began to cry.

Then, in the beautiful way he seemed to have perfected, he pulled me close and held me to his chest. As he stroked my hair, the tears slowly subsided. His very touch calmed me in a way nothing else ever had. I felt his love for me in his touch, his every action only doing more to show me how he felt. So why, when I had seen that positive, had I freaked out?

"Are you sure?" A whisper, the three words spoken on a breath, his voice shaky. Two fingers under my chin lifted my swollen eyes to meet his. In them, nothing but tenderness. And a love I could always count on.

"Yes," I whispered, feeling foolish for even doubting him a second. "I'm sure as a girl can be, but the line was nice and dark pink."

Simon's face lit up, his grin bigger than I'd ever seen it before as he crushed me to him, hugging me hard enough to steal my breath. His mouth found mine and after a few long, deep kisses, he whispered against them.

"I'm gonna be a father. My god, Elle, you've just made me the happiest man ever."

"You're...you're not mad? It wasn't planned..."

He pulled his head back with a laugh. "Hell no! Are you kidding me?"

The knot in my chest loosened just a little.

"No." I shook my head, unable to keep my lower lip from wobbling. "I wasn't sure what you'd think. I missed a few pills when..."

He caught my face in his hands.

"Never, ever think I'd be upset about that when I knew how upset you were. It takes two, you know." He grinned again. "I can't wait to be a father and I'm glad it's with you. So now you know what you have to do right?"

I bit my lip and shook my head. "No, what?"

He grinned and held up the ring. "Simon says you have to surrender and say yes, you'll marry me."

Shaking, I held my hand up as I beamed back at him. "Well in that case, I surrender to you, Simon. Wouldn't want to break the rules."

And as he slid the ring on my finger with a laugh of pure joy, I'd never felt more home in my entire life than I did in that very moment.

# EPILOGUE

### One Year Later

"I can't believe it's been over a year since you both died."

I was visiting the cemetery, crouched down between Liliana's and Stefan's graves.

*Stefan Elliot Pierce ~ Loving father, brother, son and friend* and *Liliana Nicole Pierce ~ Loving mother, daughter and friend.*

So simple, yet those words said so much.

I knew they weren't there, not really, but I still talked to them anyway.

Because both of them had brought me home.

Really, they'd both saved me because I'd still been lost and hadn't known it.

A debt I could never truly repay.

"I miss you both, so much."

I knew tears streamed down my face. I didn't care.

"Thank you for bringing me home. Without you, I'd have never met Simon and gotten married. I wouldn't have my son. I wouldn't have fixed my relationship with my mother. I wouldn't have gotten a little more time with either of you. You made me face my fears and helped me heal fully. I owe you my life."

I touched a hand to each headstone as I heard Simon approach.

He bent down beside me, our son in his arms.

Samuel Pierce Worthington, who at eight pounds and six ounces had come screaming into the world just a mere three months ago, saw me and started kicking his legs and waving his arms.

"Somebody wants his mommy," Simon said with a laugh, holding Sam out toward me.

I swiped the tears away then reached over and took him into my arms. As he clutched the front of my shirts in his tiny fists and snuggled up to me, I breathed in his wonderful baby scent. Simon put his arm around my back and kissed my cheek.

He didn't say anything else. He didn't need to.

By now, he knew me all too well.

We'd gotten married three months after he'd proposed, the ceremony taking place in Penny's backyard at her insistence. Since her family, Simon's family and mine were the only people in the world I wanted to share the moment with, it had been the perfect choice. The only choice.

Simon and I, wanting it to be a complete surprise to everybody including ourselves, had waited until the birth to find out if it would be a boy or girl. We'd discussed names but nothing had been decided until the birth. And when they'd placed our beautiful baby boy in my arms, Simon gazing down at us with a look of love that still made my heart squeeze, the decision about his name had been an easy one.

Samuel for Simon's maternal grandfather and Pierce, for the two people in the world who'd never given up on me. Who had loved me even when I'd failed to love myself.

Determined to not let that be for nothing, I'd spend my life paying it forward. It was the least I could do for the second chance I'd been given.

As Sam let out a cry and jolted me out of my reverie, Simon laughed.

"Well, Samuel says it's time for dinner and Simon says he agrees. What about you?"

With a grin, I held out a hand for him to help me stand up.

"I say it's time to go home."

And we did.

C.S. Janey

# AUTHOR'S NOTE

Elizabeth's story is just one of many women.
Women who are mistreated. Women who are
attacked, raped, abused or otherwise harmed by those
who don't care who they hurt.

It's not just women though. It happens to men,
too. To children.

It happened to me.

Abuse has lifelong effects that simply don't
matter to the abuser. Some people will be able to
'move past it' with therapy, while others end up in
worse situations, or take their life.

We should never shame victims of abuse. They
deserve a life full of happiness and should not be
looked down upon when their lives become a mess.
They should be held up, given a hand, and told how
much they are worth every single day. If you care
about them, don't give up on them - some have
darker places to come back from than others and may
simply take more time.

If you are the victim of sexual abuse, never stay
quiet. Speak out when you have the chance and don't
be afraid. More often than not, there will people who
will back you up. If someone doubts you, find
someone who will listen. Somebody *does* care and
they **will** listen.

Do what you need to do until you can say
something if you're afraid. Most of all, stay safe and
be smart.

And just remember, abuse in any form is never,
*ever* your fault.

You are worth something. You matter.
Never let a bully tell you or convince you
otherwise.

If you need help and don't know where else to
turn, contact:
National Sexual Assault Hotline at 1-800-656-
HOPE (4673)

## About The Author

C.S. Janey is a big fan of romance - writing and reading. The mother of one, she currently spends her days writing, reading, attending college to receive her BBA in Accounting, and protecting her son from himself as he pretends that he is a superhero.

*Surrender To You* is her first contemporary adult romance novel. Intended to be the first of a series, the story can be enjoyed as a stand alone. She also has many other works in progress and hopes to share them with the world soon.

Look for Grace's love story in the future, along with Yvette's.
To keep an eye out for those stories, as well as other exciting information, connect with the author at the locations below - and follow to stay up to date!

TWITTER: http://www.twitter.com/csjaney
FACEBOOK: http://www.facebook.com/authorcsjaney
GOODREADS: smarturl.it/authorcsjaney
WEBSITE: http://authorcsjaney.wordpress.com

C.S. Janey

# OTHER AUTHORS YOU MAY ENJOY

I put out a sign-up for authors to get listed here in my novel!

Below they are listed by Genre, so take a peek and discover somebody new!

## Action & Adventure
Jack Plues
Elbert Alberson (Adult)

## Chick Lit
Corri Lee (Women's Adult)
Monique Sorgen
Demelza Carlton (Adult)

## Contemporary
Christopher McGoldrick (YA/NA)

## Erotica
Beverly Ovalle (Adult)
Sarah Daltry (New Adult)
Danielle Jamie (New Adult)

## Fantasy
Bailey Ardisone
L.J. Capehart
Bill Hiatt (Young Adult)
Kate Sermon (Young Adult)
Alandra Hensley (Young Adult)

Lisa Goldman (Young Adult)
Derek White
Philip Dodd (Adult)
Susan Reid (Adult)
Jennifer Parr (Young Adult)
Lillian Bishop & Constance Williams (Young Adult)
Madeline Dyer (Young Adult)
Meg Winkler (New Adult)
Demelza Carlton (Adult)
Jessica White (New Adult/Adult)

## General Fiction
Faith Marlow
Serenity Valle
Meri Elena

## Historical Fiction
Cassandra Grafton
Laurel A. Rockefeller

## Horror
Stephen Drivick
Mark Mackey
Samuel Southwell
Lee Cushing (Adult)
Justin Bienvenue (Western)

## Humor
Dani J. Caile (Adult)
Crystal Smith-Connelly (Adult)

## Literary Fiction
Janet Moulton (Adult)

### Multi-Genre
Sofia Diana Gabel (Adult)

### Multicultural/Interracial
Stacy-Deanne (Adult Romantic
Suspense/Mystery)
Olivia Linden (New Adult)

### Mystery
Hadena James
Laurel A. Rockefeller (Historical)

### Paranormal
Jodie Pierce (Adult)
Rebekkah Ford (Young Adult)

### Paranormal Romance
C.L. Champlain (New Adult)
Sandra Bischoff

### Poetry
Mary M. Perry (Adult)
Queen of Spades
Aaron Boxley

### Romance
Devon Youngblood (New Adult)
Mellie George (New Adult)
Shirleen Davies
Sarah M. Cradit
Christa Simpson
Jackie Weger (Adult)
J.J. DiBenedetto (New Adult)

Kaylee Ryan (New Adult)
M.K. Oien (New Adult)
Tori L. Ridgewood (Adult)
Theresa Marguerite Hewitt (Military)
Nicole Tetterton (New Adult)
Michelle Abbott (Adult)
Corri Lee (Adult)
Marie Wathen (New Adult)
V. Murphy (New Adult)
Roberta Capizzi (New Adult/Adult)
Danielle Taylor
Rachel Sparks
Hilary Storm (New Adult)
Lisa Fisher (New Adult)
Karen Einsel (Adult)
Demelza Carlton (Adult)
Arabella Sheen
L.A. Remenicky (Adult)
Charity Santiago (New Adult)
Cassandra Grafton (Austen-inspired)
Clarissa Wild (Adult)
Jennifer Howard

## Sci-Fi
Margaret Taylor
Jacinda Buchmann (Young Adult)
Merita King
Ruth Silver (Young Adult)
James W. McAllister
Tuan Ho (Adult)
Arleigh Bison Westunlied

## Self-Improvement (Non-ficton)
Nihar Suthar (Young Adult)

## **Short Stories**
Samuel Southwell

## **Supernatural**
Craig Evans (Young Adult)

## **Thrillers & Suspense**
Bruce A. Borders

## **True Life**
Donald Ross

## **Western**
Samantha Livingston

## **Women's Fiction**
Mishael Austin Witty
Joyce DeBacco
Kate Warren
Patricia Mann (Adult)

C.S. Janey

Made in the USA
Lexington, KY
07 April 2014